Fatted Calf Blues

Fatted Calf Blues

Steven Mayoff

TURNSTONE PRESS

Fatted Calf Blues
copyright © Steven Mayoff 2009

Turnstone Press
Artspace Building
018-100 Arthur Street
Winnipeg, MB
R3B 1H3 Canada
www.TurnstonePress.com

All rights reserved. No part of this book may be reproduced or transmitted in any form or by any means—graphic, electronic or mechanical—without the prior written permission of the publisher. Any request to photocopy any part of this book shall be directed in writing to Access Copyright, Toronto.

Turnstone Press gratefully acknowledges the assistance of the Canada Council for the Arts, the Manitoba Arts Council, the Government of Canada through the Book Publishing Industry Development Program, and the Government of Manitoba through the Department of Culture, Heritage, Tourism and Sport, Arts Branch, for our publishing activities.

Cover design: Jamis Paulson
Interior design: Sharon Caseburg
Printed and bound in Canada by Friesens for Turnstone Press

Library and Archives Canada Cataloguing in Publication

Mayoff, Steven, 1956-

    Fatted calf blues / Steven Mayoff.

ISBN 978-0-88801-341-5

    I. Title.

PS8576.A89F38 2009   C813'.54   C2009-900710-X

For Thelma

Contents

The Most Important Man in the World / 3

The Darkened Door / 9

Danger in the Summer Moon Above / 23

The Animal Room / 25

Home, James / 37

Forgiveness / 43

Smoke and Mirrors / 47

The Bridge by Moonlight / 53

The Two Annes / 61

New Glasgow Kiss / 63

Phone Booth / 77

Elephant Rock / 83

The Same Machine / 85

Fatted Calf Blues / 93

Acknowledgements / 151

Fatted Calf Blues

The Most Important Man in the World

The King streetcar inches eastbound amidst bumper-to-bumper traffic. All the seats are taken. At every stop more people get on board and jostle for room to stand. The south side of the street, lined with chic eateries and upscale boutiques, is blocked by construction barriers where shirtless men with tanned potbellies and orange hardhats mill about carrying shovels and flags. One of them is hunched over a bone-rattling jackhammer. The broken sidewalk coughs up chalky clouds of dust into the sweltering afternoon. Even so, most of the windows on the streetcar are pushed wide open, begging for the slightest breeze.

At first no one takes any notice of the man in the ill-fitting suit standing opposite the exit doors, pressed against one of the large emergency windows. The suit is dark and looks to be made of wool, not ideal for such oppressively hot weather. His clean white shirt is buttoned right up to the stiff collar. He wears no tie.

"I'm the most important man in the world."

A young woman carrying a shopping bag from a fashionable shoe store glances over at him with a look of annoyance.

"I created the map of the human genome."

The passengers closest to him squirm uncomfortably, staring at the exit doors. I myself am sitting at the very back of the streetcar, nicely ensconced beside an open window. As usual, most of the people standing are crowded into the front half of the streetcar, leaving spaces in the rear. This affords me a better view of the man, in some ways the best view. With the bodies of other passengers between us I have an illusory, but nonetheless delicious, sense of privacy.

"I've conducted medical experiments on extraterrestrial beings."

What interests me most is to watch his face as he makes these pronouncements. Although he holds his head extraordinarily high, exuding confidence and pride, his expression is a mask of utter gravity. His voice too, clear and projected as it is, carries the sombre weight of someone who is revealing a litany of fiercely guarded secrets rather than boasting of his accomplishments. With his back against the emergency window he resembles someone who has been cornered with no hope of escape and is now forced to account for himself.

"I translated the King James Bible into binary code."

Some people are starting to smile now and of course I can't help smiling too. This tectonic shifting of facial muscles rippling throughout the streetcar awakens something in me. I can't shake off the nagging suspicion that everything he's saying is absolutely true. I think it's because, despite wearing a heavy suit in a crowded streetcar on the hottest day of the year, the man isn't perspiring one little bit. All around him people's brows are shiny with sweat, their shirts and blouses darkened by wet rings. My own scalp oozes spidery runnels down the back of my neck. But not a single drop beads the man's face or stains his clothes.

Am I the only one to notice this? Am I the only one open to the possibility that this man isn't some nutcase suffering from heat stroke? Suddenly I'm starting to feel annoyed by all these smug and sweaty dullards. I want to tell them that not only is this man playing with a full deck, he is entirely deserving of our attention and admiration.

"I cloned the Dalai Lama," he says. "I'm the most important man in the world."

Okay, maybe he didn't do any of these things. Still, it takes a fertile imagination to make up such spectacular lies. I'd even go so far as to say it takes a certain kind of genius. A few snickers and guffaws are heard, like spurts of air being pushed through fissures. He makes no acknowledgement of the laughter, staring pensively over the heads that surround him.

The streetcar lurches forward and for a moment all those standing lose their balance. They scramble to keep a grip on metal bars and leather straps. Some bump helplessly into fellow passengers. There is the odd mumbled apology carrying an undertone of spite. No one dares to look anyone else in the eye. The man finds himself splayed against the emergency window, like a dark butterfly inside a glass case. He is sandwiched in the crush of bodies. For a moment I'm worried that he'll be pushed so hard the emergency window will pop open and he'll fall out of the car into the street. It's obvious that he's uncomfortable having these bodies pressing against him. It wouldn't surprise me if he was claustrophobic and he's saying whatever pops into his head as a way of alleviating his fear. He raises his head higher and shuts his eyes. In a self-consciously flat voice, as if invoking a mantra to soothe his nerves, he says, "I can read a newspaper blindfolded. I can detect sound waves with my tongue. I can bend a lamp post with my mind."

"Okay, freak show, we get the idea."

I crane my head to see who said this. It came from somewhere closer to the front. For a second, the man in the dark suit stops, his train of thought temporarily broken. Does he feel intimidated by this outburst?

Then he continues, "I invented the days of the week."

"Shut up already!" This comes from someone different, a middle-aged woman wearing a floral print sundress. I rise slightly to get a better view and notice, in the large rear-view mirror at the front of the streetcar, the driver's face looking to see what's going on.

"I can pinpoint where the soul is located in the human body," the man says, undeterred by his detractors. "I'm the most important man in the world."

Even with the windows wide open the afternoon heat is concentrated inside the streetcar. We're sardines roasting inside an oversized tin can. Suddenly I see someone shoving the man in the suit. He braces himself against the window to keep his balance. Then, from out of the crowd, a fist punches the man in the shoulder. Another hand violently tugs on his jacket lapel. The man makes no move to protect himself.

"I predicted—"

The rest of his declaration is drowned out by the machine-gun stutter of a jackhammer on the sidewalk. Billowing grey dust wafts through the streetcar windows. Everyone starts to cough, covering their mouths and eyes. But the attack on the man accelerates as somebody pulls his ear one way while someone else twists his arm the other way.

"... the most important ..." I hear the man say amidst the chaos.

I know I should do something, pull the emergency cord or yell for them to stop. I sit and watch, feeling safely distanced from him, buffered by the bodies between us, weighed down by a moral inertia. I'm not entirely sure what I'm witnessing is real. Amidst the heat and dust the whole thing has the aura of a dream.

I find myself standing, edging past the bodies of other passengers in slow motion as I make my way toward the man. I have no rescue plan in my head, no real idea of what I'm going to do if I can get close enough to him. At first the bodies are obstacles in my way, but as I continue to squeeze through they begin to act as a propulsive force, thrusting me forward until the man is right there in front of me. His arms are being pinned behind him and I look into his terrified eyes. I'm repulsed by the way he's grinning at me, the corners of his mouth twisting from horror to ecstasy. I can tell he's about to make another one of his pronouncements as I smash my fist in his mouth, loosening a front tooth. Blood is streaming down his chin and I dig my fingernails into his temple before he is jerked aside, beyond my grasp.

The streetcar stops and the doors open. The man is being forcibly pushed toward them, stoically bearing slaps and punches as he passes through the gauntlet of passengers. Someone gives him a shove and he stumbles down the steps. The doors close and the streetcar jerks forward.

I can see him through the back window, limping in a daze between the slow-moving traffic and the construction barrier blocking the sidewalk. The shoulder of his jacket is torn, the sleeve dangling partway down his arm. His shirt is open at the front, most of the buttons having been ripped off. The top button is still intact, holding together the stiff white collar, which makes him look like a hobo priest. He spits blood and I can clearly make out four red gashes on his temple. My fingernails have blood on them and I stuff my hand into my pocket.

As the streetcar clatters on I think about trying to make my way back to my seat, but I see it's already been taken. No matter. At each following stop the bell rings. A reminder of something, perhaps to pick up a newspaper or a carton of milk. Or a signal that tells us it's okay to start forgetting. The crowd thins out as passengers swiftly and silently disembark.

The Darkened Door

The note is written in a fluid, neat hand using violet ink from a fountain pen on unlined paper, possibly from a small sketchbook. It has been folded once and taped to Roy and Kendra's apartment door, between the brass numbers and the peephole. They have returned from grocery shopping.

> I have been sleepwalking through a mist of uncertainty, guided by a restless intuition. Torn between cowardice and courage, every step plagued me with doubts. Am I a fool? Is it possible that you feel the same as I do? It is only now, here at your door, that I awake to an inner light, trusting the one thing that has always kept me going—I love you more than life itself.

"I don't recognize the handwriting. You?" Kendra thrusts the note in Roy's face. He is kneeling before the open refrigerator struggling with the crisper drawer. He pushes her hand away.

"This bloody thing gets stuck all the time," he says. "I'm going to see Mrs. Prowse on Monday. They should give us a new fridge."

"They're not going to give us a new fridge just because you have an ongoing battle with the crisper. You have to lift it a bit then pull."

"Well, I shouldn't have to. We pay enough rent for this hovel."

The drawer slides out. Roy continues to put the groceries away, the kitchenette being too small for the two of them to do it together.

"It's kind of poetic," says Kendra. "What about that new cashier at the restaurant? Didn't you say she wrote poetry or published a book or something?"

"I think she organizes poetry slams. What about it?"

"Maybe she wrote this. You said she was kind of sexy."

"I said she was kind of freaky. But I guess sexy too, if you're into Goths."

Kendra imagines Kabuki-white skin, black lipstick and hair, multiple piercings. "Listen to some of these phrases. '*Mist* of uncertainty.' 'Every step *plagued* me with doubts.' Sounds kind of Gothic to me."

"Weeping Jesus!" cries Roy. "I don't believe this."

"What? I'm just saying ..."

"Kendra, have you seen these plastic bags? They're all bunched up so you can hardly open the drawer." Roy pulls plastic bags from the drawer until the kitchenette floor is mostly covered.

"What is it with you and drawers? Aren't you the least bit curious about who left this note for you?"

"There's no end to these damn things. It's like the black hole of plastic bags." He begins to smooth down each one, replacing them neatly in the drawer. "Anyway, what makes you so sure it's for me? Maybe someone left it on our door by accident."

"'It is only now, here at your door, that I awaken to an inner light ...' It doesn't sound like they left it by accident."

"It could be a prank. Somebody with too much time on their hands."

"Well, that explains it. Now we can get back to our thrill-a-minute lives."

"You want adventure, Kendra? It's a stalker. He's obsessed with you."

"Or you," she says.

"Or both of us. Let's really make it kinky."

"*Kinky?*" Kendra laughs. "What Sunday morning sermon did you get that from?"

She leans diagonally within the kitchenette's narrow entrance, taking up the entire space. Roy presses down on the bags, stuffing them into the drawer.

She folds the note five or six times, flattening the edges with the nails of her thumb and forefinger, until the paper is nothing but a small blank square. Unfolding it, she notices how the creases break up the message.

-king through a mist-

She holds up the note. "The handwriting is very neat, which makes me think it might be a woman."

-tuition. Torn between cow-

"But you have neat handwriting," she continues. "So it could be a man. Although that doesn't rule out it being for you. Who knows? Maybe your little locker room fantasy is coming true."

"Very funny," says Roy.

"Nothing to be ashamed of. If I remember correctly, you strip down to your socks, but won't take them off—"

"Okay, that's enough."

"—until two guys hold you down while a third removes them only to reveal your toenails are painted candy pink. But you never actually told me what happens after that."

"I'm sorry I ever told you any of it," says Roy.

Leaning against the kitchenette entrance, she slides down the frame until she is sitting. "Makes me wonder what kind of things you haven't told me."

-fool? Is it possible that-

"You mean things like: the creative impulse is linked to the sexual one. Eh? That kind of thing?"

"Oh, for God's sake, Roy. That was over a year ago. We promised—you promised never to bring that up again."

-your door, that I awake-

Roy snatches the note. "What's it say here? Something about

cowardice? Yeah, 'Torn between cowardice and courage.' Wasn't Mister Over-A-Year-Ago afraid of leaving his wife? How do we know this isn't from him?"

"He doesn't have that much initiative."

"How could I forget." Roy stares at the plastic bags on the kitchenette floor. "You made the first move, didn't you?"

-to an inner light trust-

"Why are you bringing this up again?"

"No, Kendra. Why are *you* bringing this up again?"

"What do you mean?"

"You couldn't wait to tell me after your last affair."

"It wasn't—"

"Whatever." Roy brandishes the note at her. "So is this it? Another one? Is this your way of rubbing my face in it again?"

Kendra grabs the note and springs to her feet. "Screw you!"

She stamps her foot on the garbage pail's pedal—flipping the lid open—crumples the note and flings the wad of paper inside, then spins around to storm off as the lid *chomps* shut.

Roy kneels on the linoleum, listening to her stomp around in their bedroom, sliding dresser drawers open and shut. Then the squealing hinges of the front closet's bending doors, followed by the tangled clanging of coat hangers. Finally, their front door slams shut. All is quiet. He finishes smoothing out the last of the plastic bags and pushes them down into the drawer.

Kendra crosses the corner of Bloor and Yonge, oblivious to the amber light. The odour of spicy grilled sausages from a street vendor mingles with gassy exhaust fumes. Her stomach squelches between hunger and nausea.

Once inside the glass doors of the HMV store, she rides the escalator to the upper level. Displays of newly released CDs are surrounded by signs declaring BUY 3 GET 1 FREE.

She wastes no time in methodically flipping through the first row in the rock section. Halfway through, having made it as far as *Alice In Chains*, she is approached by one of the store clerks.

"Are you looking for anything special?"

She looks up. "Oh my God. Gary?"

"Hey ... Hi there ...?"

"Kendra."

"Right, sorry. Kendra. How's it going?"

She folds her arms and smiles bravely. "Since when do you work here?"

"Coupla months ago. Just doing it part-time. What about you?"

"I'm still temping on and off. Flexible hours."

"Same here," says Gary. "I don't want to get dug in."

"Amen to that. How's the band?"

"On hiatus. Andy's on the road with Alanis."

She leans in closer. "You doing any writing?"

"Got a couple of tunes. Lyrics are a little slow in coming."

"You need lyrics?" she says. "I'd really love to—"

"Oh, check this out." He points upward as music blasts through the store. "This is the new one by The Hives. This really kicks ass."

She pretends to listen. "Oh, yeah ... cool."

"Anyway, nice seeing you again."

He is about to walk away when she grabs his arm. "Hey listen, whatever happened to that song we wrote?"

His eyes dart from side to side. "Song?"

"At that Muskoka workshop?"

"Oh right, that. I don't know. I played it for the head honcho at Nova Publishing—what's his name? —Freddy. He liked it but he said it wouldn't fit in their catalogue."

"It was a damn good song. You even said Pam liked it."

"I don't remember saying that." He starts to shuffle through the CDs, pretending to put them into some kind of order.

"How is Pam anyway?"

"Um ... we're kind of taking a break right now."

"Sorry to hear that."

"We kind of lost touch with each other. It was like we were sleep-walking through the marriage."

She looks at him pointedly, cocking her head, wondering if she heard right. "Sleepwalking?"

"Yeah, if you know what I mean."
"I think so. *Sleepwalking. Through a mist of uncertainty.*"
"Through a what?" His brow is a ropy knot. "I didn't say that."
"No," she says flatly. "I guess you didn't."
"Are you okay? You look kind of pale."
"I don't know. Something's going on."
"What do you mean?"
She begins to sing: "*I've been sleepwalking ... sleep ... walking ...*"
"Listen, my manager isn't too cool with people singing in the store. She's looking this way right now."
Kendra raises her head and belts out even louder: "*I've been sleepwalking ... Sleepwalking through a mist of uncertainty ...*"
"Look, Kendra, this is not cool."
"Why the hell not, *Gare*? This is a music store, isn't it? Shouldn't I be free to make music here?"
"You're starting to freak out the other customers. I'm sorry, but I have to ask you to leave. Let me walk you to the door."
"Let go of my arm."
Gary raises his hands. "Look, I'm sorry. I don't want any trouble. I just got this gig."
"Then what was all that crap about not wanting to get *dug in*?"
"Hey, look, I just—"
She crows for the whole store to hear. "Look at you, *Gare*, you're *dug in* right up to your scrawny pencil-neck!"
"C'mon," he pleads. "I just need you to leave peacefully."
"Don't worry, I'm going. But before I do I've got a lyric for you."
"I don't want to have to call—"
"*I got my dick in my hand,*" she drawls in her bluesiest growl and grabs her crotch. "*But I'm just a toady for the man.*" She punctuates the last word by flipping him the bird high in the air. "There it is, *Gare*, from me to you. Peace out."
She wheels away from him and strides toward the escalator.

Kendra returns to the apartment sometime after 4:00 when she knows Roy is starting his shift at the restaurant.

Once inside, she heads straight to the garbage pail. Brown banana peel, folded wet coffee filter with dark grounds spilling out of it, empty yoghurt container with a curled section of its tinfoil lid still attached.

No crumpled note.

With the tip of a fingernail she flips over the serrated top of a tomato paste can. Roy must have taken it out while she was gone. What the hell did Roy want with the note? That prick. Pretending he didn't care who'd left it. Pretending it didn't mean anything.

She rifles through his underwear and sock drawers. Maybe he took the thing with him to work to confront the cashier.

Roy and the cashier?

Kendra grabs her guitar, which is leaning against the dresser, sits on the bed and strums a couple of chords. "*I have been sleepwalking,*" she sings. "*Sleepwalking through a mist. Sleepwalking through ...*"

She can't sit still. When she gets the idea for a song in her head, she calls it *creative agitation*. She slings the guitar strap over her shoulder, walking into the living room, opening the window, lighting a cigarette. Strumming and pacing. Waiting for it to piece itself together.

So the fucker has known all along who the note is from.

Why else would he soil his immaculate hands to retrieve it from the garbage? Fucking around behind her back. Getting his revenge. Yeah, so she had a stupid one-night stand. With pencil-neck Gary of all people. They'd written a good song together at the Muskoka workshop. That's how it goes sometimes, the excitement of two people creating something. There's this residual energy you have to work off somehow. *The creative impulse is linked to the sexual one.* How long had Roy been waiting to throw that back in her face?

"*I have been sleepwalking,*" she sings to the walls. And not suspecting a thing. Why did she tell Roy about Gary? He would never have known. She wasn't interested in Gary, even if he hadn't been married. And he wasn't interested in her. Gary being afraid of leaving his wife was just made up, something to tell Roy.

Because Roy had no idea whatsoever. Why did she find that so intolerable, Roy not knowing about her and Gary's meaningless fling? She told herself it was because she couldn't stand seeing Roy being made a fool of, even by her. She had pleaded with him to forgive her. Not just for being unfaithful, but also for telling him about it.

She stops pacing. The ringing of the last chord hangs in the air. She stares at the bottom drawer of the kitchenette counter. She puts down the guitar and kneels on the linoleum, pulling the drawer out entirely, turning it upside down and shaking it. White plastic bags flop onto the floor, some are shiny square pancakes stuck together, others bloom open on impact.

A dizzy ghost flutters down.

The note.

It has been smoothed out, but the paper still shows creases.

She cradles the guitar in her lap, lights another cigarette and reads the note over and over, imagining Roy making love to someone. The cashier? Strange arms and legs, thin as elongated shadows, wrapped around his naked body. The hurt sinks into her and slips out again—a red-hot needle stitching every line onto her stretched-out heart.

> *I have been sleepwalking,*
> *sleepwalking through a mist of uncertainty,*
> *guided by a restless, a restless intuition ...*
> *It is only now, here at your door*

The Belair Bistro in Yorkville is a popular and chic eatery, but this evening only three out of the twenty or so tables are occupied.

Roy, looking trim in pressed black trousers, crisp white shirt and pearl-grey vest, stands by the cashier's station.

"I'm going on my smoke break, Roy," she says. "Wanna join me?"

The cashier, all in black, has spiky magenta hair. A silver cross dangles from a thin expensive chain, small wiry hoops pierce each eyebrow and a stainless steel labret protrudes from under her bottom lip. There are several ornate rings around her tapered fingers and skull-shaped studs in her earlobes. Her pale skin has a slightly bluish tinge.

"You know I don't smoke, Bella," he says.

"You're looking a bit tense tonight."

"I've never seen the place this slow. I've only waited on a handful of customers since five o'clock."

"So then there's nothing stopping you from joining me. There's no rule that says you have to actually smoke on a smoke break." She nods toward the other waiter who loiters by the kitchen. "Costa can watch things."

Bella opens the fire door onto a narrow alley and lights up a Dunhill.

"Actually I'm kind of glad it's slow," she says. "I'm hoping to leave early. There's a midnight launch at the Three of Cups for a new zine called *Orphans of Morpheus*. It's about the culture of insomnia. All the artwork and poetry was created under the influence of severe sleep deprivation. I stayed up three days and nights on espresso and amphetamines writing my poem, *Rocket By Baby*."

"Sounds intense." He smoothes down his vest. "I hate it when it's slow. No tips. Besides, I prefer to be worked off my feet rather than doing nothing."

"Idle hands are the Devil's playground and all that?"

"If you like."

"You know I do, baby."

He shakes his head. "What do you see in that whole spooky Goth thing?"

"It's fun." Wisps of smoke drift from her carved nostrils. "For me it holds a kind of campy spirituality. A black and white aesthetic. No grey areas."

"Life is nothing but one giant grey area."

"That depends. If you look close enough grey is really made up of black and white dots, like Lichtenstein in monochrome. The sacred and the profane in pointillism. It's like Oscar Wilde said: *We are all in the gutter but some of us are looking at the stars.*"

High up between shadowy rooftops, an ebony strip of sky sports a glittering pattern as dramatic as diamonds on velvet.

"The stars are nothing but illusions." Roy waves a dismissive hand. "They burnt out long ago but the light is only now just reaching us slowpokes here on planet Earth. All those pretty tinkling things up there are really ashes of the past."

"I had no idea you were such a nihilist." Bella aims a perfectly lacquered purple fingernail at him. "You're giving me gooseflesh."

Roy grins, cheeks and neck prickling hotly. His nostrils fill with the warmed-over fruitiness of burgeoning trash bags along the alley: a déjà vu of retrieving the note from the wastebasket earlier that afternoon. He straightens the already impeccable cuffs of his shirtsleeves.

"Someone left a note on my door today." His polished oxfords confront him with his own reflection.

"Oh?"

"A love note." He hears his voice disappear into the alley. "Unsigned."

"Ooh, a secret admirer. Any idea who it is?"

"Well, Bella ..." He screws up the courage to look at her. "I actually thought it might be you."

"Trust me, Roy, if I left a love note on your door you'd know beyond a shadow of a doubt that it was from me."

"*Be my bloody valentine* written in real blood?"

"For starters."

"I guess you think I'm a real dope."

"Some people, yourself included, might think you're just an uptight, super-efficient nonentity." She traces a fingernail along his stiff collar. "But I know there's more to you than meets the eye. That's because I have something no one else has."

"What's that?"

"Bella-Vision!" Her dramatic eyes peek out through splayed fingers. "It cuts through that ocean of grey conformity and sees your black and white huddled masses yearning to be free."

"I'm glad you find this so amusing."

"Serious frivolity is my weapon of choice."

"In a way I feel like I've been violated by that note," he says. "Invaded."

"Maybe you should think of it as a visitation."

He rubs his chin. "That sounds even more ominous."

"It doesn't have to be," she says, taking a final drag, savouring it like a fine wine. "It could be benevolent."

"How am I ever going to know one way or the other?"

She flips the butt into the alley. "Even black has to meet white half way if they're going to make magic together."

"Or before they slide into greyness."

"There is such a thing as grey magic," she says. "A way of seeking the extraordinary in the mundane."

Without waiting for a reply she resumes her post behind the cash register. His fingertips tingle, reminding him of how safecrackers use sandpaper to heighten sensitivity. He steps out into the alley to extinguish Bella's still-burning cigarette and takes one last look up at the star-glistened strip of nighttime sky. It reminds him of a dazzling runway. A jumping-off point.

Roy returns home at midnight, annoyed to find the front door of their building partially open. People don't care. They come in the building and are either too much in a hurry or too lazy to make sure the door is closed properly. This is probably how whoever left that note slipped in.

Two women sit on the sofa in the lobby, each seemingly oblivious to the other, except that they are holding hands. They remind him of wax figures. He has an urge to call out or wave his arms to wake them from their reverie. Instead he watches the elevator numbers as they count down. When the doors slide open he catches another glimpse of the women's clasped hands.

When he arrives at his floor he fishes for his keys. How quiet it is tonight. No voices, not a TV or radio coming from any of the other apartments.

He stands at his door with key poised, stopping to study the space between the brass numbers and the peephole. There seems to be some discoloration. He rubs at it with the side of his hand, then licks his thumb and rubs harder, but to no avail. Was it there before this morning? He imagines it might be residue left from the note.

The apartment is dark except for the light over the stove. He sees the empty drawer on the counter and the floor covered with plastic bags—eerily shapeless under the stove light. Kendra's guitar is leaning against the sofa. At the top of the neck a piece of paper is wedged between the strings. It is the note sticking out like a stiff flag. *I hereby discover this land in the name of ...*

Kendra pretends to be asleep and feels Roy slip into bed. The moon's pale shimmer frosts the edges of the bare window. Through the slits of her eyes she can make out his image in the half-darkness.

"How was work?"

"Busy."

"Was Vampira on tonight?"

"It wasn't her."

"How do you know?"

"I just do."

Kendra sits up. She reaches for cigarettes and a lighter on the side table. The flame casts weary shadows under her eyes, illuminating the loll of one breast and its indented nipple.

"So is it someone I know?" she asks.

Roy takes the cigarette from her. Kendra is surprised. He isn't a smoker, except if they go out to a nice restaurant for dinner. He puffs a couple of times. The glowing end flares and wanes like a distress signal.

"I'm not having an affair." He hands the cigarette back to her. "If that's what you mean."

"But you know who left it." She stubs the cigarette out in the ashtray on the side table. "Don't you?"

She slides down, moving her hand along his thigh and rolls his foreskin between her fingers. The underside of her arm detects a panicky tightening of his stomach muscles.

"Don't you?" she repeats.

She straddles him, bracing her hands against his chest, rocking steadily. His hips push up toward her and she collapses on top of him. They lie motionless. The brittle measure of his breathing through clenched teeth. She nudges her face against his and feels his cheeks wet with tears.

It is only now, here at your door,
that I awake to an inner light,
trusting the one thing, the one thing
that has always kept me going—
I love you more than life
more than life itself ...

Kendra hasn't listened to the tape since she made it a week earlier, the day she wrote the song. The guitar is tinny and her voice sounds far away. A relic of the past. She punches the mini-recorder's *off* button and rewinds the cassette. She lights a cigarette and pulls the bed covers up to her chin. The closet door is ajar. Sunlight streams through the bare window and catches the hard curves of empty hangers.

Roy stands at the foot of the bed, zipping up his suitcase. "I'll come back for the rest of my stuff in a few days."

"You might change your mind," she says and immediately regrets it.

She reminds him of someone convalescing from a long illness, someone whose dishevelled vulnerability appeals to your sympathy and at the same time repulses a part of you.

"I could understand you leaving if there was someone else," she says.

"Someone else?" He pretends to check the top of the dresser. "For you or for me?"

"Either."

"I'd probably be more tempted to stay if there was someone else."

"I don't understand." She shakes her head.

"It's like that part of the note. 'Torn between cowardice and courage.' It made me think of your ... *fling*. I tried to understand why you told me about it."

"I wish I never did. Why are you throwing all this back in my face now?"

"All that stuff about the creative impulse being linked to the sexual one. It's a restlessness in you. Maybe it's easier for me to forgive that sort of thing if I've never felt it. Because I'm supposed to be the calm one, the rock."

She sits up abruptly. "But you feel it now?"

"When you first threw the note away I was relieved. Good riddance. But later I closed my eyes and saw the note taped to our door and remembered that I hadn't actually seen it the first time. I was too busy with the groceries. It was you who saw it first and took it off the door."

"So?" The sheet is bunched in her fists. "Who cares who saw it first?"

"I felt cheated that I hadn't. That's when I took it out of the garbage."

Roy picks up his suitcase. Kendra watches him leave. After a moment she hears the front door close and the click of the lock. She wishes they had bought shades for the bare window and slumps further under the covers as the brilliant morning fills every corner of the room.

Danger in the Summer Moon Above

It is a dangerously clear night. Too many stars and a razor-sharp moon. Me and Terry hop over fences and crawl on our bellies through backyards. Fresh-mown grass pinpricks through my T-shirt. We call ourselves the Danger Twins. Our faces and arms smeared with dirt from Terry's mom's garden. Terry is eleven, a year older than me. He leads the way. We crouch in the shadows away from back porch light bulbs burning yellow through mosquito clouds. Holding our breaths perfectly still at the slam of a screen door. Avoiding patio chairs and plastic pools. Passing unseen beneath windows lit only by a milky blue TV glow.

I started being friends with Terry at the beginning of summer. A week after my mother died. She had tuberculosis. When I told Terry about that he just shook his head and frowned. "Tough break, man." We went riding on our bikes and later met up with another kid we both knew from school. This kid was telling us how his mother had just come home from the hospital with a new baby sister. Terry put his arm around me and explained to the kid, "His mom just kicked the bucket." It was a weird thing to say. In one way it hurt, even though I knew Terry wasn't trying to be mean. But in another way it put a real picture in my mind. A way that described how I was feeling. I could see this metal bucket lying on its side. The hard curve of the rim showing the emptiness of it. That hollow feeling in the pit of my stomach. After that we spent practically every day together.

"This way," Terry whispers. We wriggle through an opening of some high shrubs. A twig scratches hard against my arm.

"Shit!"

"Shut up, you knob," he hisses in my ear. "You want her to hear us?"

I have no idea where we are. Some backyard and it's real dark. Only one window has a light on. There's a woman sitting in front of a mirror brushing her hair. She's wearing some kind of bathrobe. Her hair is long and red and she brushes it very slowly. This is the woman Terry has told me about. The cashier at the supermarket who smiles at him. I can see her lips moving like she's talking to herself in the mirror. It's so quiet I can hear only the two of us breathing. The woman stops brushing her hair and looks out the window. She isn't looking at us, but it's like she knows we're there. I feel another kind of hollowness inside me.

The woman moves away from the window. The light goes off. "Let's go," Terry says. But I don't move and he puts his arm around me. I can't stop shaking. "C'mon, man. It's okay." Above the house, the moon has turned us both into shadows.

The Animal Room

One of the rats has died overnight. As soon as I step out of the elevator I breathe in the first strong whiff. Damn nasty. No time to change into my whites. I head straight into the Animal Room. I can almost see the stench slithering around the corners of the whitewashed walls, rubbing its back against the fluorescent lights, wrapping itself around the stainless steel faucet. Not the usual stink of caged rats, that's second nature now. I don't even notice it anymore. This is worse. The stench of death.

Most of the cages are wire mesh and fit like drawers into either side of four tall iron racks, so there's no quick way to find the dead animal. I have to check every cage. For the uppermost ones I balance on my toes, craning my neck to peer in. For the lowest cages I have to squat down and these days that's harder on the knees. The worst thing is being all out of breath. I cover my mouth and nose with a handkerchief. The stench is starting to make my eyes burn.

Some of the rats sleep with fat hairless tails curled around them. Some drag tumours back and forth, like prisoners with their balls and chains. They can smell the dead one and it agitates them. Their gnawing and scratching turn more feverish.

I finally find the dead one lying on its back, baring long sharp teeth. An imitation of fierceness. The paws resemble little bony pink hands, holding onto nothing. The stomach's been eaten away. Now the stench is unbearable, coiled in its nest of wet entrails.

I put on rubber gloves and fetch a heavy plastic bag from a cupboard in the far corner of the room. Two other rats are curled up together in the cage, sleeping off their late night feast. They stir slightly as I slide the cage open and in one motion take out the dead one, drop it into the bag and push the cage shut. The two others lift their heads, sniffing the air, then go back to sleep.

I seal the grooved strip on the bag and drop it into the freezer out by the elevator. The freezer is more than half-filled with dead rats and mice. You can barely see them because the plastic bags are clouded by the last of the animals' body heat, turning into what looks like icy cataracts.

My office is right next to the Animal Room in a small L-shaped area at the very top of the Strathcona Building. There's also a storage room with a large iron vat for cleaning cages. Beside it is a teaching lab where Dr. Kilmer, the head of the Anatomy Department, often brings her students.

After I change into my whites and replace my leather street shoes with rubber-soled canvas runners, I fill the kettle and plug it in.

Before becoming Animal Room Technician here I worked for six months at the McIntyre Medical on the far side of the campus. Over there I was tending other animals that the university used for research. Dogs. Cattle. Monkeys. It was hard. I was depressed a lot. A dog is a smart animal. Even a cow. You can see something in those brown eyes. Once they brought in a gorilla and I had to wrestle him down so they could sedate him. After the injection he started to calm down and looked right at me. I expected to see some kind of anger or hatred in his eyes. But it was worse. There was a look of confusion and then surrender. After that I started to lose my appetite and found it hard to sleep.

That's why I transferred here. I only have to deal with the rats. They're easier to deal with. I can handle them. There's nothing to see in their beady red eyes. That's because they're only vermin, scavengers fit for roaming the sewers or the alleys. At least here they have some use. Here they're helping mankind in some way.

Once the kettle starts to whistle I drop a bag of peppermint tea into my mug and pour the hot water. I take a moment to let the peppermint steam rise into my face. Something to cleanse away all traces of the stench from my nostrils. Clear it out of my head.

The rest of the morning is spent changing the plastic cages that hold pregnant rats and newborns. I'm lining them with clean shavings when Annie comes into the Animal Room. I call her Annie Cornflowers, which embarrasses her. The colour of her eyes reminds me of the cornflowers I used to see in the fields around my grandmother's farm near Trois-Rivières, where I spent most of my summers growing up. I used to travel there by bus on my own. The rest of the time I lived with my mother in a tiny apartment in the north end of Montreal.

Annie has finished her first year of pre-med and is doing some work in the Anatomy Department over the summer for extra credits. She always crinkles her nose in an unpleasant way when she comes into the Animal Room and says she'll never be used to the smell. Her voice is very soft. I think she's a little afraid of me. She sometimes seems embarrassed and can't look me in the eye. I'm sure she sees this gross, hulking body and tries to hide her pity and contempt. Still, I like the way Annie blushes easily. Her neck is delicate as a tendril and glows a deep rose colour in contrast to her crisp white lab coat.

"What can I do for you this morning, Miss Annie Cornflowers?" She speaks down at her shoes. "I'm sorry, Annie, I didn't hear you."

"You said you would help me inject two of the rats for my experiment."

"Did I?"

She looks worried but says nothing. The poor girl is still quite nervous around the animals and hasn't learned to hold them properly with a firm grip.

"You'll have to wait until I've finished doing these cages."

She nods and looks relieved.

I transfer one of the expectant rats from its soiled bedding into fresh shavings, then snap on the metal lid and slide the water bottle back into the groove. The rat immediately starts to push the shavings to one side of the cage.

"Doesn't it hurt her when you hold her by the tail?"

Whenever Annie watches me change cages she asks me this. She worries too much about the rats and I try to settle her fears. I always try to be patient with Annie Cornflowers.

"Not if you move the animal quickly. If you just hold it, it will start to struggle and possibly injure itself. It could also bite you."

The next cage holds a rat that gave birth the day before. There are seven newborns. "It's important to transfer the mother first. If you go for the babies the mother will attack to protect them."

After I put the mother into the clean cage, I tell Annie to move the newborns so she can get a feel for handling the animals.

"Oh no, I don't want to hurt them," she says.

"You won't hurt them. Give it a try."

She looks into the cage. The newborns are pink and hairless with eyes still closed, yipping like tiny squeaky hinges. Annie's mouth purses into a nervous frown as she picks one up between her finger and thumb and quickly drops it into the cage with its mother.

"No, no, no. You can't do them one at a time or else you'll be here all day. Just scoop them up into your hand."

"But—"

"Go ahead. Don't be afraid."

Annie positions her hand beside the newborns, carefully sliding it into the shavings and under them. She lifts her hand and the remaining six are cradled in her palm. Squirming little sausages, shivering and crying, huddling together for warmth. There's both fear and tenderness in Annie's eyes at the way the newborns cluster and seem to fuse into a single pulse. A wriggling pink muscle. A shapeless beating heart.

"Okay, now put them into the cage with the mother."

She does not move, staring at the newborns in her hand. Their cries are growing louder so I figure it's up to me to do something. I take hold of her wrist and guide it to the cage and the newborns drop safely onto the shavings with their mother. Maybe I grabbed her wrist too hard or turned it too sharply because she looks at me in alarm and pulls her hand away.

"What were you waiting for?" I try to laugh, but there's anger in my voice. "You were in a dream world."

She opens her mouth. Saliva glistens on her teeth. Tears are forming in the corners of her cornflower eyes and she rubs her sore wrist.

"I didn't mean to grab you so hard. Here, let me see your arm."

She takes a step back.

"You shouldn't be scared of me, Annie Cornflowers. I would never hurt anything as beautiful as you."

"But you did."

"I'm sorry. It was an accident. Just let me see it. I promise not to touch."

She won't come near me and continues to rub her wrist. I try to look suitably penitent, but now she is walking along the rows of racks, still cradling her wrist in her other hand, as if holding a wounded bird, and peers into each cage. So solemn and curious. So innocent. I feel like an intruder and wonder how to gain her trust again.

"If you want I'll help you with your animals now. I'll even do the injecting so you can see how it's done."

"I know how it's done." She won't look at me, but keeps inspecting the cages. "I've seen you do it before, the way you hold the poor rat hard by the scruff so it can't move and then jab the needle in."

"But if you hold it right the rat isn't hurt. And the needle just pricks for a moment, like when you get a shot at the doctor."

"Do you really think they like it in these cages?"

"Why not? There's always enough food, always fresh water. Besides, they're bred in captivity. Cages are the only home they've known."

"Then why are they always trying to escape?" she asks with her head cocked to one side. Her innocence now tinged with sarcasm. I can't help taking this personally.

Her wrist must be better now because she's not holding it anymore. Instead she runs her index finger along the cages. Softly at first, but then she does it harder, her fingernail against the wire making a clacking noise. I tell her to stop because the noise upsets the animals. She waits a moment and starts it again, soft at first, then harder and louder than before. I'm afraid she's going to take the top of her finger off. When I make a move towards her she backs away and gives me a hard stare, showing she's not scared of me. And I believe it. This is a new side of Annie Cornflowers I've never seen before.

"You're supposed to be a professional," I say. "We're all here to do serious work. So do you want help with your animals or not?"

"Never mind that. If you really cared about them you'd set them free." There is a sincerity in her voice that breaks my heart, as much as I am shocked by the suggestion.

"That's crazy. I can't set them free. They're in my charge. I'm responsible for them."

I don't like the way she is wandering around the cages. I take a step towards her but she disappears behind one of the racks, spying on me through a space between the cages.

"You're responsible for their lives, for their health," she says. "Even for their deaths. The burden falls squarely on your shoulders. You are their god."

I move around the rack but she's too quick and runs the other way, taking refuge behind the next rack over. I try to be silent and fast, but she's younger and more agile. My forehead is damp and I can feel my heart pumping madly. She can see my every move and laughs childishly, amused as hell by this cat-and-mouse game.

Then one of the racks starts shaking. Annie is pushing one end of it from side to side, trying to topple the thing over. The racks are on wheels so they can be moved around, but they're heavy, even for a strong burly guy like me.

"Stop that now," I shout.

"If you want ... me to stop ..." She's gasping, barely getting her words out. "You have to promise ... promise to free the rats."

She gives the rack one last push and I see it teeter for a moment. I rush and lean all my weight until it's steady again. I turn to Annie who is backed against a wall, panting like a cornered animal. I approach slowly, trying to regain my own puff.

"This is over now." I tell her this gently.

"Don't come any nearer."

"I'm sorry I grabbed your arm. I don't want any trouble."

"Leave me alone!" She makes a run for the door. For a minute I'm stunned, unsure of what to do. When I check the hall and down the narrow stairway there's no sign of her anywhere.

The large binder with the breeding schedule is open on my desk. I look down at the straight columns of dates and cage numbers, but in my head I'm going over the whole business with Annie Cornflowers, rerunning it like a movie and stopping at certain moments, then playing it back again. Perhaps it never really happened at all, only in my head.

There is a sound and I look up to see Dr. Kilmer politely knocking even though the door is open. I didn't hear her come up the stairs. The wavy fullness of her white hair always reminds me of goose down. Her eyes are serious but kind behind rimless glasses. They give her expression the tranquillity of a windless lake.

"I wanted to talk about the breeding schedule with you." She points at the binder. "You must have read my mind."

She pulls up the only other seat, an iron stool next to the mini-fridge. I make a motion to stand. "Maybe you'd be more comfortable in my chair."

She raises her hand. "This will be fine."

"One of your rats died last night. I found it this morning."

She nods with a kind of dispassionate melancholy. I think of how understanding she was during my interview when I was looking to transfer from the McIntyre Medical. She had nodded the same way after I told her how difficult it was for me there. I think at some point I made her smile, recalling the summers I spent on my grandmother's farm, how I learned to love animals even when I was slopping out the stalls. I discovered at a young age that the most honest smell in this world is manure. That made Dr. Kilmer shake her head, but laugh out loud nevertheless.

While we are looking over the breeding schedule she's telling me about her ideas to expand the Animal Room and modify our system. As much as I'm trying to pay attention I keep thinking I should say something about Annie Cornflowers. Dr. Kilmer knows how trustworthy I am, how vigilant I am about my job. I've never let her down. If she found out in some other way about what happened this morning I could get into trouble.

"You're not listening, are you? You seem to be in another world."

"I'm sorry, Dr. Kilmer. I'm not sure what's wrong with me. I slept badly last night."

"Is something bothering you?"

"Nothing really. Just a strange dream I had. It woke me up in the middle of the night and I couldn't get back to sleep."

This is true. I had totally forgotten about the dream until this very moment, but now it comes flooding back into my mind like misty moonlight.

"What was the dream?" She is perched on the stool, expectant as a child ready to hear a story.

"You see, there was this travelling fair that came every summer to Trois-Rivières and set up not far from my grandmother's farm. It had games and rides and candy stands. In my dream it was deserted. I had the whole place to myself and I couldn't believe my luck as I walked around. But all the candy stands and game kiosks were locked up so I couldn't help myself to the food or the prizes. The gates to all the rides were also locked.

"The only ride that was open was the carousel, which had always been my favourite. I scrambled up the ramp, but once on the ride I noticed that all the wooden horses had been replaced by giant white rats. Their mouths were open with long wooden teeth painted yellow and their wooden tails were painted pink and curled into spirals.

"I was walking around when the carousel suddenly started to move. I tried to jump off, but the next thing I knew I was sitting in one of the swan boats, except it wasn't a swan. It was an upside-down rat with its paws straight up in the air. The stomach was dug out and the inside was lined with a very plush red material. I wanted off, but it was moving too fast and I had to hold onto the metal pole to keep from falling out. Then I woke up."

The way her eyes search mine unsettles me. I look down at the page in the binder. The columns seem narrow, like underground tunnels. I hear Annie Cornflowers' voice in my head, something she said this morning: *Then why are they always trying to escape?*

We return to the breeding schedule and even as I pay close attention to what Dr. Kilmer is saying, another part of me can't help but listen for the elevator and glance occasionally at the stairway.

At 4:30 I'm wheeling the racks around so I can mop the floor. Sometimes I fall into a trance, pushing the wet mop around, how the soapy water gives the cement floor a sheen under the fluorescent lights, bringing out the tiny dimples and crevices. The surface of another world.

I glimpse a flash of movement at the corner of my eye. The constant vigilance of making sure everything stays in order plays games with my mind. Sometimes the vision is just a figment of my imagination, but sometimes it's real. Even though I try to ignore it, concentrating instead on dragging the mop across the floor, my attention is like an agitated compass needle that keeps being drawn to a corner of the room. And there it is: one of the rats has crept out of its cage. Not an adult, but probably a couple of weeks old with a new soft coat. A white cotton ball.

I carry the mop and metal bucket to the storage room, empty the bucket into the iron vat and go to my office. From the cupboard over the sink I retrieve the plastic pail with the lid that snaps on. There's also a small pile of old newspapers and I grab a couple of sheets, lining the inside of the pail. In the mini-fridge is an open can of ether and I splash some evenly over the newspaper. Then I press the lid on so it's airtight and carry it into the Animal Room.

The rat is cowering behind a wheel of one of the racks. It scurries behind another wheel. What I need to do is flush it out into the open. I nudge it with my foot and it dashes to a corner. At least it's a bit more out in the open now, a little easier for me to scoop up. The rat is very still. Only its stringy tail stiffens and quivers, preparing to make a move. My shadow darkens its sky.

I grab it up in my fist and balance myself with my other hand against the wall to straighten up. The pail is next to the sink. With one hand I pop open the lid, trying not to breathe in the ether. Then I drop the rat in the pail and reseal the lid. I hear the desperate scrambling, the sound of tiny claws scuttling through ether-soaked newspaper.

I go to the sink to wash my hands. The water rings loudly in the stainless steel basin. I roll the soap well between my palms and concentrate on lather. I feel weightless, same as when I was a boy on the farm, watching my grandmother prepare to kill a chicken. Her face would be a mask of determination as I stood by. A silent witness to something brutal and necessary. My ears would echo with the sharp whack of the blade against the wooden block, the spurting blood and frenzied headless body. Afterward I would go stand by the road staring at the edge of the fields fringed with wildflowers, my skin all tingling and purified.

I turn off the tap. There is still the tiniest whiff of ether in the air. The sound coming from inside the plastic pail has stopped now. Everything is too silent.

There's a faint bristling on the back of my neck. I turn and she's standing there in sweater and jeans, no lab coat. A small beaded purse is slung around one shoulder. It looks small enough to hold a wallet, I can't imagine what else she would keep in it. She looks lost, as if she walked into this room right off the street without thinking.

"Is it dead?" She's looking toward the pail. Her voice is low and meek.

"Yes." I pull a couple of paper towels from the dispenser and dry my hands. "How is your wrist?"

She rubs her forearm in what looks to be an automatic response, maybe from the power of suggestion. She quickly stops and clasps her hands, looking embarrassed. "It feels okay."

I go to the cupboard for a small plastic bag to put the baby rat in. When I turn around she has pried the lid off the pail and is looking inside. For a minute I wonder if she's going to start crying. Actually her face has no real expression except for a slight wrinkle on her forehead. Her whole body is still and solemn as if witnessing some great mystery—similar to when she was holding the newborns—but this time there is more a quality of abstractness, something unnameable.

"Why did you have to kill it?" She asks this the way a child might ask why the sky is blue.

"I had no other choice. It escaped from one of the cages, but I don't know which one. These animals are bred specifically for certain experiments."

"What are you going to do with it now?"

"Put it in this bag and then into the freezer."

She puts her hand into the pail and takes out the dead animal and holds it in her palm. A white puffball lying so still it might as well be asleep. "I wondered if you were going to report me to Dr. Kilmer," she says.

"I should have."

"Why didn't you?"

The empty plastic bag feels conspicuous in my hand. "I don't know. I think I felt responsible somehow, like I let things get out of control. Like the whole job suddenly got too much for me. Dr. Kilmer trusts me. I didn't want her to know I let her down."

"But you defended your post, didn't you?" She smiles shyly and a strange fog of emotion wells up behind my eyes.

"The truth is I was afraid you would come back," I say. "And I didn't know what I would do. If I would turn you in or not."

One finger strokes the dead puffball in her hand. "Are you afraid now?"

I take a step toward her and hold out the plastic bag. She slips the baby rat into her tiny purse and zips it closed. I know this is something I shouldn't allow, but make no move to stop her.

I ball up the bag in my fist and stuff it into my pocket. She turns and walks out of the Animal Room. The door closes behind her and she looks back through the square glass. I feel a terrible emptiness. Her face seems distant except for those eyes: the brilliance of cornflowers shining in a field seen from the window of a passing bus.

Home, James

"How come you never learned to drive before?" Myrna asks as she reaches for the passenger seatbelt.

"I'm not really sure," I say. "I guess I never really felt the need to before now."

I pull my seatbelt across my chest and slide the metal piece into the buckle. Myrna does the same and our belts click in unison. She's wearing a summer dress and sandals. The garnet polish on her big toenail is starting to chip.

I fit the key into the ignition.

"Okay, it's really simple," she says. "Just turn the key and press lightly on the gas pedal until you feel it catch."

We're in an empty parking lot. I do what Myrna tells me and wait a moment to get accustomed to the engine's vibration thrumming through me like nervous laughter. Myrna instructs me on how to shift into DRIVE. I slowly take us around the parking lot.

"You're doing well. Make a turn at that pole. And don't forget to signal."

I drive us around the parking lot as Myrna gives me hypothetical situations to deal with, such as coming to an intersection where another car has the right of way or what to do at a stop sign. Now and then I pass the exit that leads to the street and wonder what it would be like to take the car into real traffic.

"I'll bet Al must think it's funny you teaching me how to drive," I say, trying to get that second nature feel of talking and driving at the same time. "I mean me learning after all this time."

"Al took Janie up to his mother's farm for the long weekend. I don't go near the place. Allergies."

As a final test Myrna makes me back into a parking spot. I turn the ignition off and we sit for a moment.

"So? How did it feel?"

I light a cigarette. "Weird. It was like this recurring dream I sometimes have, where I'm driving a car, even though I don't know how to drive. But somehow I know what to do. It's a strange feeling. Sort of like being helpless and powerful at the same time."

"You want to take us home?"

"And what if we get stopped? I don't have a licence."

Myrna unbuckles her seatbelt, leans over and takes a drag off my cigarette. Smoke drifts from between her lips. We kiss.

The strap of her dress slips off her shoulder. I glimpse the curve of her breast. Reading my eyes, she brushes her lips close to my ear. "Home, James."

I start the car and drive to the parking lot exit, pausing a moment to let some cars go by. A police cruiser passes and one of the cops looks right at me.

"In this dream are you alone or is there someone in the car with you?"

I don't answer. Taking a deep breath, I steer the car onto the road. In the rear-view mirror I see myself grinning anxiously, as if I know at any minute I could wake up.

"How come you never learned to drive before?" Al asks as he reaches for the passenger seatbelt.

"I'm not really sure," I say. "I guess I was always scared to do it for some reason."

I wait to hear the click of Al's seatbelt before pulling mine across my chest and sliding the metal piece into the buckle. Then I fit the key into the ignition. Al is staring straight ahead, a million miles away. There are dark circles under his eyes.

"Okay, I'm ready."

We're in an empty parking lot. Al patiently instructs me on the turning of the key while gently pressing my foot against the pedal. I notice the lower half of Al's jaw starting to tremble.

"Should I put it into DRIVE now?" I ask, my hand hovering over the stick shift.

"Yeah. Easy. Give it a bit of juice, but don't gun it. That's good."

I take us around the perimeter of the parking lot, nervously aware that Al's attention seems to be focused on some inner distraction.

"I'll bet Myrna must think it's funny you teaching me how to drive," I say, trying to get that second nature feel of talking and driving at the same time. "I mean me learning now and all."

"Myrna thinks I took Janie up to my mother's farm for the long weekend. She never goes because of her allergies."

"Then what are you doing here?"

He stares grimly at the windshield, like he's considering whether or not to put his head through it. "I think she's seeing someone."

I press my foot on the brake.

"Don't stop. Keep driving or else it will look suspicious."

I continue and Al has me perform simple manoeuvres such as signalling to turn left, then right, then backing up.

"What makes you think she's seeing someone?" I ask.

"She told me."

"What do you mean, she told you?" I can barely bring myself to make eye contact with him.

He won't look at me either, which makes me feel uneasy until I realize he's genuinely embarrassed. "She was talking in her sleep."

"What did she say?"

"'Home, James.'"

"What?" I nearly collide with a stray shopping cart.

"That's what she said. 'Home, James.' She kept saying it over and over."

"I don't understand."

"It was the way she kept saying it. Kind of breathy, like she was ... you know."

I stop by a row of well-spaced cement pylons. For a moment we're both silent. The engine is idling, shuddering through us. I fidget with the rear-view mirror and our eyes accidentally meet in the glass. Al clears his throat and instructs me to wind in and out between the pylons as an exercise in handling the wheel. I manage to do it without scraping any paint off the doors. Then I cut the engine. Al is weeping softly.

"It'll be okay," I say, lighting two cigarettes at the same time and handing one to Al. "It might not be what you think."

"I've been having this same dream where I'm following her. She's up ahead in our car, sitting on the passenger's side. There's someone else driving. A man. I keep driving faster to catch up to them but the guy speeds up just enough to always stay ahead of me."

"Look, I have to get going." I unbuckle my seatbelt and open the driver's door, expecting to change places. "Could you drop me off at my place?"

Just as I'm about to get out he grabs my arm. "I don't want to drive," he says.

"Well, I can't. What if we get stopped? I don't have a licence."

"I'm afraid," Al says and stares at me with red, teary eyes. It's a weird look he's giving me, sort of pleading and accusing at the same time. "Of what I might do."

Something in me goes cold, but I close the door and do up my seatbelt. I start the car and drive to the parking lot exit, pausing a moment to let some cars go by. A police cruiser passes and one of the cops looks right at me. He makes a point of showing his gun, pretending to check the clip.

"In this dream, do you ever see who's driving?"

Al doesn't answer. I take a deep breath and steer the car onto the road. In the rear-view mirror I see Myrna hiding in the back seat. She holds a finger to her lips. I keep my eyes ahead, wondering which one of us will wake up first.

"How come you never learned to drive before?" Janie asks as she reaches for the passenger seatbelt.

"I'm not really sure," I say, helping her with the buckle. "You really think you can show me?"

"I've watched Mommy and Daddy lots of times. I know what to do."

I smile to show I have every confidence in her. She's wearing a pink T-shirt and jeans cut off at the knee. I imagine this must be how Myrna looked at that age.

We're in an empty parking lot. I'm about to put the key in the ignition when she tugs on my sleeve. "Uh, uh, uh," she says in a sing-song voice, pointing to her seatbelt, then to mine.

"Just testing you." I pull the strap across my chest and click the metal piece into the buckle. I can feel the edge of the strap biting into my shoulder.

Her instructions are sharp and to the point. "Put the key in. Now turn it. Press the gas pedal. Pull the stick to D for DRIVE."

I do all these things and soon I am steering us around the lot.

"Okay, pretend there's a dog trying to cross the road. Now here's a green light. Oops, it just turned red."

"What happened to amber?"

She giggles and shrugs her shoulders. "Look out, you almost hit that lady."

I veer sharply and Janie squeals with delight.

"I'll bet your mom and dad must think it's funny you teaching me how to drive," I say, trying to get that second nature feel of talking and driving at the same time. "I mean you being eight and all."

"I dunno. They think I'm at my grandma's farm."

"Don't you think they're going to be worried about you?"

"I dunno."

"They could be out looking for you at this very moment."

"But I'm here with you."

I'm stunned by the way she says this. The sheer innocence of it opens my eyes to the gravity of the situation, the onus that's been put on me. A moment ago we were having such fun, I didn't have to think about anything. Now panic is starting to set in my bones like rigor mortis. Both hands are locked onto the wheel in a death grip. My only thought is to park the car in the next space I come to so we can just sit there, quiet and safe, until someone comes to get us.

But as I'm about to pass the parking lot exit some reflex makes me steer out onto the street. I merge seamlessly into the flow of traffic.

"What if we get stopped?" says Janie. "You don't have a licence."

I get out a cigarette and put it in my mouth. I'm about to light up when I notice Janie's disapproving stare. I leave the cigarette unlit and try to savour the bittersweet hint of nicotine through the spongy filter. It's like breathing through a straw. Everything seems to be happening in slow motion and instantaneously at the same time. Up ahead is an on-ramp for the highway that leads out of the city.

"So," says Janie. "How does it feel to be really driving?"

"Weird," I say. "I've never really gone beyond this point before."

In the rear-view mirror is a police cruiser. One of the cops is talking on his radio. Al and Myrna are in the back seat. Myrna is crying and Al is leaning forward, saying something to the cop who's driving. They're closing in behind as I make the turn onto the on-ramp.

"Where are we going?" Janie asks.

I don't answer. The sun glares against the centre of the windshield and I feel like I'm struggling to access some long-lost memory. Hoping to steer toward that place where we can all wake up for good.

Forgiveness

In Cedar Dunes Provincial Park Carl waits out the storm in his car. He writes a letter to his wife as great blinding sheets of gunmetal rain pummel the roof and windshield.

Then the storm is over, as quickly as it had begun, leaving a disquieting cobalt sky. He puts the letter face up on the dashboard and gets out of the car, leaving his keys in the ignition and the doors unlocked.

There are wooden stairs leading to the beach, but Carl trudges over sodden grassy dunes, ignoring the signs that say KEEP OFF. There's no one around and the tall lifeguard chair is empty, it being too early in the season.

The leaden sea churns low cross-current waves as he walks along the russet stretch of wet beach. Close to the water he picks up medium-sized stones, which he stuffs into his coat and trouser pockets, feeling a gradual confidence with the growing weight of them. The water is tinged red for quite a way, showing how far one can go out before it becomes too deep. He'll probably have to wade a good ten or fifteen minutes before it's over his head. He never learned to swim and can only hope the stones will do their work so the sea can take him quickly.

In the early days he and Lucille used to come here, especially after an argument. Some couples like to make up in the bedroom, but he and Lucille always found a quiet walk along the beach more conducive to forgiveness.

Around eight months ago she told Carl about the affair she was having. He was devastated, but believed their marriage could survive this rough patch. After twelve years of being married he still loved her. Nevertheless, she left him and went off to live with the other man. Since then, Carl's phone calls to Lucille have always started with the best of intentions, but inevitably deteriorated into desperate pleading and ended with recriminations and tears. His heart constantly throbbed with a darkening ache.

That's when he began to go to Cedar Dunes on his own, searching within himself, hoping to find a way to forgive her. He believed that if he could do this she would miraculously return to him. His recurring fantasy was that he'd be walking along the beach and there she'd be, coming toward him. They would find each other like castaways washed up on the same shore.

That hope was finally quashed when Lucille called to say she wanted to marry the man she was living with and hoped Carl would not make complications. Yesterday he was served with divorce papers. He has them folded up in his inside coat pocket as he walks along the edge of the shore where the tide's rolling lip teases the soles of his shoes.

Past the West Point lighthouse, Carl sees something in the distance—a small statue, maybe something kids have made out of the wet sand. Approaching for a closer look, he catches a movement, amazed to find that it's alive: a hawk standing perfectly still on two twig legs. Glittering foam washes over its talons then ebbs back to the Atlantic. The feathers are drenched and it seems to be in a state of shock, unable to move. Obviously battered by the storm, or possibly dragged under by a wave, then spewed out onto the shore.

Carl tests how close he can get until the hawk lowers its head, wary eyes fixing him with a cold yellow stare—a warning not to come any nearer. Drenched or not, he believes the bird means business and so he stays where he is.

"I tried so hard to forgive her," he says and looks around to see if anyone is watching. Only the bird. Its scrutiny makes him feel petty and selfish.

He remembers all those hours trying to comprehend why this was happening. All she could ever say was that she fell out of love with him. Like the victim of some kind of accident. He believed she felt bad about it, but he knew that could never be enough, could never bring him to acceptance. He knew the fault lay within him.

It strikes him that this is no ordinary hawk. Battered and bitter, jaundiced eyes filled with terror and rage. Carl feels as if he is looking at the mirror image of something struggling inside him.

The sun nudges the clouds aside and the hawk spreads its wings under the golden warmth—then takes to the air. Carl shields himself with his hands and stumbles backward, falling to the ground with a sharp thump to the small of his back. The hawk's shadow passes over him, obscuring the sun in a split-second eclipse. Then he is momentarily blinded by white brilliance. Shading his eyes, he searches the sky but the hawk is nowhere to be seen.

He struggles to his feet, the stones in his pockets reminding him why he came here today. The weight of them seems to push his heels into the wet sand. He brushes himself off, as if at any moment Lucille might come strolling by. But she won't. He knows that now. The stretch of beach is as bereft of her image as the open sky is of the hawk's.

He thinks about the letter that's sitting on the dashboard of his car. Some of the words he used: *despair, choice, peace*. He thinks of the unlocked car doors and the key in the ignition. He may as well be dead already. *Forgiveness*. He remembers that was how he ended the letter.

He looks up into the sky again, hoping for some sign of the hawk. Its disappearance has left him numb. A vital part of himself having let go. He wonders what has been left and touches the outsides of his coat pockets where the stones bulge through. Such a foreign presence. And yet they feel like an integral part of him now as he stares out toward that place where the sea and the sky become the same.

SMOKE AND MIRRORS

The club is full tonight. It's my first smoke break in four hours. Besides waitressing, I did a few table dances. All those jokers peeling bills off a wad like Kleenex while I'm shaking it in their noses. Their hooded bloodshot eyes: curious moles peering out of tunnels, staring straight up inside me, yet another strange tunnel. The only payoff for them is slipping a fiver under my garter. Jimmy the doorman keeps an eye out that their hands don't roam any further. So far there's been no real trouble, but I've had to call him over a couple of times. Usually when the customer sees this brick shithouse in a suit coming toward the table he gets the message quick.

Weird to think it's almost two years since I graduated from theatre school. Feels like a lifetime away. I haven't exactly had a whole lot of luck since then. Did some extra business in a couple of films, a bit of summer stock in Orangeville and some leads in community theatre. Of course there's no money in the community stuff, but you get a chance to ply your craft, like I didn't pay through the nose to do that for three years at the prestigious Canadian Academy of Theatre Arts.

Mostly what I've been doing is auditioning my ass off. Sure, there

Fatted Calf Blues

was some training in CATA on how to audition, how to prepare yourself. But nothing prepares you for the endless rejection. The smiling faces that look you over and think *no way* before you even have a chance to open your mouth. I tell Sandy to send me out for everything. She's not a bad agent. Used to give me good advice on how to dress, who to kiss up to. Lately though she doesn't seem to have much time for me. If she knew about this gig she'd drop me in a second. Part of me keeps waiting for that phone call, telling me to find another agent because she only handles serious actors.

Denis the deejay gives me the nod. After three months here, I'm doing a turn on the stage, which means a few more bucks. Denis got me this gig. He's friends with Kenny, the guy who does my head shots. I couldn't pay for the pictures so we worked out a barter thing where I did a little modelling for him instead. Nothing graphic, just tasteful shots for his private collection. Denis saw them and said he could get me into the club if I wanted. At first I said no, but then I thought about it. You get leered at and hassled in any waitressing job. The way I see it, at least here I'm getting paid for the hassle. At least I know what I'm up against.

I stash my tray behind the bar and make my way toward the stage. I can't help hearing Madame Voronov's voice in my head. *Look your body. Drop shoulders. Chin up.* Her class was the first of the day. She always told us dancing is acting. We're playing a part. Usually she made us do a waltz or a tango. I don't think this is what she had in mind. Still, when she told you to do something you did it. The iron rod of my spine straightens, making me taller. I've seen some of the girls up there. Christ, it's like watching the living dead. Stoned, most of them. Addicts. None of that shit for me. This gig is definitely temporary. Just to pay the rent until things start going my way. The minute I feel myself sliding I'm outta here.

Denis gives me an intro. "Please put your hands together for the lovely Ruby."

The back wall of the stage is made up of mirrors. I'm bathed in pink light, supposedly to make me look sexy. I look like one of those plastic blow-up dolls. Shiny and bloodless. The glare of the light makes the floor darker than I expected. Stale clouds of cigarette smoke hover around all those waiting faces.

Denis starts the music we picked out. Hot salsa. Not too fast but the beat is right there, as steady as a hand guiding the small of my back. Supporting me.

Chin up. Drop shoulders. Look my body.

As part of my stage costume I've chosen a skimpy vest with long buckskin fringes. I flip the fringes over my head and take off the vest in a neat swirl, whipping the stage a couple of times to get their attention. Look at them: vacant leers and the same old world-class stud fantasies. Time to play the matador now, waving the vest around like a cape. *Toro, you ring of sad-eyed bullocks. Toro!* Some guy points his fingers from the top of his head, mimicking the horns of a bull, and gets out of his seat, moving toward the stage. I'm about to signal Jimmy, but instead I whip the fringes real hard on the stage, right where he's heading. The force of it sends him reeling back to his seat. *Olé!*

Holding the vest in front of me I try to undo my bra clasp with one hand. I practised this a few times in my apartment, just to see how hard it would be, and got it on the third try. Circling the stage I glimpse the mirror. The pink light is making the blue smoke go all purplish. For a moment I dance with my own reflection, the way I did last night, trying to imagine how it would feel up here. In a way it's exactly what I expected, the smallness of the stage and the tension of being of trapped. Caged in. But now, looking in the mirror, everything seems different. A satiny curtain of smoke divides me from them, and at the same time enshrouds all of us together. There's this fine line of distance and intimacy. All I want is to be able to step through the mirror and walk that tightrope.

Finally, I undo the clasp and toss the bra aside. I turn toward the crowd, twirling the vest in front of me in a circular motion. The fringes start to spin with all eyes following until I toss the vest over my shoulder. The crowd hollers and whistles and I let the din wash over me in echoing waves. I think about that time in scene study class when I mimed a striptease as Ophelia. *O heat, dry up my brains! Tears seven times salt, burn out the sense and virtue of my eye!*

Everyone called it brilliant.

The salsa rhythm pops and sizzles through the speakers, daring me to prowl the edge of the stage. All last night in bed I lay awake trying to mentally prepare for this. I thought about approaching it as a rehearsal or maybe an audition. I even tried to imagine it as some kind of research for a part I might be playing in the future. Unsure of where to turn, I peer through the swirls of gauzy smoke, narrowing my eyes to mere slits, letting everything blur until all the faces seem to merge into one, except for that familiar face out at the back of the room.

Sandy.

She stands near the door. Her face is devoid of all expression.

My first instinct is to run to her, grab her hand and get the hell out of this place. I want to throw myself at her feet and beg her forgiveness. Swear that I'll get a legit job if she gives me a second chance. My heart is hammering in my ears, all the blood flowing throughout my body in no particular direction.

Then I turn to the mirror and see only myself. This eerie calmness— a single coil of sweet white smoke—fills every inch of me. I slide the thong down my legs and feel myself entering the watery glass—the razor-edged coolness of a still lake. From inside the mirror I turn, standing naked, and face them all. They're banging the tables with beer glasses, howling and screaming and slapping their hands together. Sandy is nowhere to be seen.

Denis' voice booms over the sound system, "Let's have a big hand for Ruby."

My time is up, but I don't move. The pink light is turned off and I feel invisible, lost between the darkened mirror and the dissolving folds of smoke: a mere shadow of my former self from a minute ago, when I existed.

Again I hear Denis saying, "Thank you, Ruby," as if he's encouraging the audience to applaud some more. But I know he's really telling me to leave the stage and get back on the floor. Everyone is ordering more drinks and eyeing the other girls.

I gather up my stuff and mentally go over my to-do list.

Get some new head shots.
Learn a new audition piece.
Find a new agent.

I remember one afternoon in voice class during my first year. The teacher was leading the class in an exercise to feel our diaphragms. I suddenly felt an overpowering sadness and began to cry. The whole class stopped to watch. My eyes stung with shame. And pride. The teacher explained that the crying was connected to my breathing and called it a breakthrough, rewarding me with a comforting hug. Everyone else came over and touched my shoulder sympathetically. I could feel their seething jealousy. I was making progress. Paying my dues. I could feel their hands on me as if they hoped some of it would rub off on them.

But I don't feel like crying now. There's nothing to cry about.

Mirrors break.

Smoke clears away.

Only the applause is real.

The Bridge by Moonlight

Elva Peart sits on the porch of her cottage in Augustine Cove, watching the fading bloom of sunset behind the Confederation Bridge. Her grandson kneels at the edge of the lawn and plays with his truck on the gravel road, which winds past the other cottages, leading to the main paved road.

"Rennie, it's past time you were in bed."

He keeps his eyes fixed on his truck, moving it back and forth within a small rut he's dug in the gravel. "I want to be up when my mum gets here."

Elva's daughter-in-law was supposed to have arrived an hour ago, but when Elva called earlier, Trace's cell phone was off. What was the point in having a cell phone if you were going to leave it turned off? One of those pay-as-you-go plans. Elva knew Trace was watching her money and didn't want to use up the time on the phone. Emergencies only. Still you'd think she'd call to let a body know she's running late, that she's okay.

It's barely a year since Elva's son died. Cut off by a drunk driver on the double highway through Edmunston while hauling potatoes to

Quebec City. Rennie had just turned three. Trace scarcely makes ends meet with what's left of the insurance cheque.

Elva likes it at night when the lights along the bridge turn on. She remembers when they were still building the bridge, how it was going to connect the island to the rest of the world. It'll be faster than the ferry, they said. Better for trade and tourism. A new era of prosperity.

Elva can't see the cars from here. For all she knows, Trace might be driving across the bridge at this very moment.

"Come on, Rennie. It's too dark for you to be out now."

"But I don't want to miss my mum."

"If you want to stay up you have to sit on the porch here with me."

The boy gets up, leaving his truck in the gravel rut. He stretches his short legs to climb the wooden steps and then pulls himself up onto Elva's lap. She rocks the two of them on the little porch swing.

"How come my mum has to keep going to Moncton?"

"She's doing some work there."

"With that man?"

"Yeah," she says, shadowing the word with a drawn breath.

"He's a friggin' poo-head."

"You know I don't like that language."

"He yelled at me once," says Rennie matter-of-factly. "When I dripped ice cream on his car seat."

Elva kisses the fine tangle on top of her grandson's head. Rennie yawns and presses his cheek against the crook of her cradling arm. Under the shimmering new moon the bridge is nothing but a spine of stars linking to an invisible mainland.

The phone rings and her first instinct is to let the machine take it. The boy's getting comfy, why disturb him? But it could be Trace. A cold flicker starts something coiling inside her. Remembering the phone call from the police telling her about Stevie's accident.

Rennie is sliding off her lap now. "I want to answer it."

"You stay here on the swing."

"If it's my mum I want to talk to her."

The screen door slams behind her as she strides down the hall. She manages to get it just before the third ring, beating the machine. It's Trace. Right away Elva can tell she's not calling from her cell phone.

"Where are you?"

"Still in Moncton." Her speech is slightly slurred. But there's something else in her voice. Something percolating between the words.

"Have you been drinking?"

"Just a couple glasses of champagne."

"Why, is it New Year's Eve over there?"

"Don't be cross now. And as a matter of fact we are celebratin' somethin'. But it's a surprise. I'll tell yez tomorrow."

Elva listens for the squeak of the porch swing outside. "Rennie's been waiting up for you." She tries to keep her voice hushed. "Poor mite."

The sudden clatter of the screen door makes Elva almost drop the phone. Rennie comes running part way across the hall and slides the rest of the way on the Indian throw rug, pretending it's a flying carpet, the same as what he saw on the *Aladdin* DVD his mother bought him.

The rug was a birthday present to Elva from Stevie. He'd picked it up at a roadside shop on the way back from one of his hauls.

"Lemme talk to my mum!"

"You put that rug back properly first," snaps Elva, more harshly than she intended. She doesn't like the idea of letting the boy talk to Trace when she's in this condition. Not that she gets that way often, but Elva knows well enough it's not all business when Trace is in Moncton. Elva's mind is a blank as she tries to think of an excuse not to let the boy have the phone. But he has straightened the rug and is now pulling on the coiled telephone cord.

"What did I say about grabbing?" She reluctantly gives up the receiver to his little hands.

She's only half listening to the one-sided conversation. Rennie wanting to know when his mom's getting back and why does she have to keep going away. The automatic responses pop in Elva's head, but her mind is mostly thinking about what Trace said about a surprise. Elva didn't like the sound of that. It had all the earmarks of Trace going ahead and doing something foolish. Like taking that part-time job in Moncton. Driving out there every other week to do the books for that real estate salesman. Staying in some apartment he rents for her. What did Trace say his name was? Davis. Separated from his wife in a pig's eye. Foolish girl. With her skills she could have easily found a job on the island. Even Elva's nephew Kyle got something at the Tax Centre in Summerside after passing the test on the third try.

Elva notices a top corner of the screen on the outer front door has come loose, curling over to reveal a perfect triangle of emptiness in contrast to the grey wire mesh.

"My mum wants to talk to you." Rennie holds up the receiver like a tiny weightlifter hefting a small barbell. Elva takes it from him.

"What's this surprise you're going to spring on us? I'm sure I've had enough surprises to last me my life."

"Like I said, I'll tell yez tomorrow. I already told Rennie that that's when he's gonna find out."

"Well that should keep him up all night, thanks very much."

"I want to tell yez together in person." She lets out a throaty giggle and tells someone on her end to cut it out.

Elva looks down at Rennie then quickly looks away. It's on the tip of her tongue to tell Trace to grow up. "And what time can we expect you tomorrow?"

"I'll probably leave here around noon. So I should be there probably by two."

Famous last words, Elva thinks as she hangs up the phone, then regrets thinking it. She goes over to the door and tries to push the drooping corner of the screen back in place but it curls over again.

It's too late to give Rennie a bath so she undresses him and pulls on his Spiderman PJs, then changes into her nightie. He wants to sleep in her bed. She doesn't want him to make a habit of it but relents. It's supposed to be a grandmother's privilege to spoil her grandchild, but Elva feels she should give the boy some discipline, what with his mother being away so much. She doesn't want to call Trace a bad mother, but sometimes the girl should know better.

"My mum is bringing me back a surprise. She said so. I think it's going to be a new truck. D'yah think so?"

"No point worrying about that now. If you're going to stay in this bed you have to go to sleep. Now."

He rolls on his side and nuzzles his back against her side. Just like Stevie used to do when he was that age. In a few minutes his steady breathing fills the darkness like the slow hiss of a radiator. Reassuring in a strange way. It is she who lies awake, staring out the window at the lights on the bridge.

Trace holds out her hand with her wrist slightly limp, the better to display the ring on her finger. It is a slender band made of white gold with a diamond chip embedded in the middle. Elva eyes it suspiciously, although a part of her is impressed. The clankety-whirr of the bent blade on the electric fan's metal grate seems to be mimicking her mental process, so many things running through her mind. The two of them are sitting at the kitchen table with tall glasses of iced tea. Rennie is on the porch playing with the racing car Trace has bought him.

"He took me out to The Keg and gave me the ring before the dessert came. It was in a beautiful velvet box. Who could eat after that anyway?"

"And he actually proposed right there in the restaurant?" asks Elva, trying to get the facts straight in her head.

"His divorce came through last week. I didn't even know. He was keeping it as a surprise."

"Doesn't waste time, does he? You'd think a man would want some breathing space after the end of a marriage."

"Davis isn't like that," says Trace narrowing her eyes. Her knowing smirk embarrasses Elva. "He loves being married. It's his wife who divorced him. His ex-wife I mean. She only married him for his money anyway. She never cared about making him happy."

Their conversation is interrupted by the slamming screen door and the heavy stomping of small bare feet on the hallway's wooden floor.

Elva calls out, "What have I said about running inside?"

"You listen to your Nana now," Trace adds.

Rennie stops just before entering the kitchen. His two small hands grasp onto the entranceway frame with feet firmly planted in the bottom corner of the frame, dirty toes scrunched upward. He swings back and forth like a rickety gate with his head stretched back, trying to catch the breeze off the electric fan.

"How come you're not outside playing with your new car?" Elva asks.

"I want a drink."

"I beg your pardon?"

"I want a drink," he says. "*Pleeeeeze.*" He stretches his head back farther so that the word barely squeezes out of his little throat.

"You're going to fall some hard if you keep doing that," says Trace. "Come sit on your mum's lap and have a drink. I want to show you something."

Elva pushes her chair back and Trace looks at her. "Don't go," she says.

"Do you think now's a good time?" Elva asks. "Maybe ..."

But Trace only nods to say it'll be all right. Rennie scampers onto his mother's lap. Elva reaches for his juice cup on the counter and pours some iced tea into it. She finds she has to hold the plastic thermal pitcher with both hands to keep it steady. She screws on the juice cup's spouted top and hands it to Rennie.

"What do you say to Nana?"

"Thank you," he says and pops the spout into his mouth, sucking hard like a baby with his bottle.

Elva watches as Trace waits for Rennie to finish drinking. She feels as if she's not in the room, like she's looking in on them. Checking to see how mother and son are getting on. Always at the ready to rush in just in case there's a problem of some kind. Making herself into a bridge between them. Now that Stevie's gone. Like it was yesterday. Rennie on Trace's lap. *Daddy's not coming back from this trip. He drove his truck straight up to Heaven.*

Rennie stops drinking but holds on to his cup with both hands. Trace holds up the ring. "See? Mumma got a present too. It's some pretty, isn't it?"

"Where'd you get it?"

"Davis gave it to me. You remember Davis? The man I work for in Moncton? Remember that one time he took us for a drive in that big car of his?"

Rennie nods, staring at his juice cup.

"Didn't you tell me he bought you an ice cream cone?" Elva asks. Rennie looks at her. She smiles back, trying to reassure him, feeling utterly helpless.

"I don't want you to go to Moncton again," Rennie says and sticks the spout back in his mouth.

"I got to go next weekend. I got a job to go to. But I tell you what. This time you can come with me to Moncton. Davis has a nice big apartment there. That's where we'd stay. Me and you. Would you like that?"

Rennie stops sucking on the juice spout. He puts the cup down and reaches his arms out to Elva. Her instinct is to pick him up off Trace, but she does nothing. Her hands are folded numbly on her lap. She feels like her arms have been cut off.

"Honey?" says Trace. "You didn't answer me. Would you like that? Me and you living in Moncton?"

Rennie shakes his head vigorously. Trace has her arms around his little belly and he starts to squirm, trying to wriggle off her lap, his arms still outstretched to his Nana.

"Lots of toy stores in Moncton," says Trace, not loosening her grip on him. He starts to whine. Elva shoots her daughter-in-law a look. Trace loosens her arms and Rennie hops down, goes over to Elva and drops his head in her lap.

"Why don't you go out and play with your car," Elva says, stroking his hair. It's getting long, but she can't bear the idea of cutting it, it's so soft and cool like a sudden breeze. She watches Trace circling the diamond chip on her ring with her little finger and can't help feeling bad for her.

Later that evening Elva gives Rennie a bath, puts him in his PJs and tucks him into his bed.

"I want to sleep in your bed again," he says.

"I let you last night. We're not making a habit of it."

"Then I want to sleep in my mum's bed."

"Not tonight," says Trace. She is standing by the doorway and steps into the room. "Let's show your Nana that you're a big enough boy to sleep in your own bed. Now give me a kiss good-night." She kneels by the bed and offers her cheek. He wraps his arms around her neck and smacks his lips loudly against her puckered mouth.

After Elva reads him a story and turns off the light, she goes out to the porch where Trace is sitting on the steps smoking. A suitcase and a smaller valise are nearby.

"What are you doing with those?" asks Elva.

Trace blows out smoke toward the bridge. She doesn't look at Elva. "I called Davis and told him we're coming tomorrow."

"What's the hurry? Rennie'll come around, but you need to give him some time."

"The sooner he gets used to it the better. He'll be okay once we're there."

Elva sits on her swing. Trace's clunky old Bonneville is parked on the gravel road. Elva notices Rennie's toy truck from where he left it yesterday. It's lying on its side nearly under the Bonneville's front left tire.

"Not long after Alvin died I took Stevie on a trip to Halifax to see his Auntie Soph, Alvin's sister." Elva stares at the back of Trace's head and the trail of smoke that seems to be rising from it. Trace has probably heard this already, but Elva doesn't care. "Drove there with Alvin's brother in his pick-up. There was no bridge then, of course. We had to take the Borden ferry over to Cape Tormentine. Stevie loved the ferry, loved looking out over the water. Soon as we got to the other side all he wanted was to ride back again."

Trace flicks away her cigarette butt and the red glow arcs into the night, as fleeting as a shooting star "Don't you think I miss him too?" she says. She still won't turn around and Elva understands it's because she's crying. Then Trace gets up from the steps and carries the two suitcases to the car.

The bridge is lit up now. All the lights, except one. Elva focuses on that dark space, a deeper absence intensified by the surrounding lights. She rocks on her swing, the metal hinges complaining softly. The moon plays hide-and-seek, weaving in and out of invisible clouds.

The Two Annes

Samson Grief sits at a café patio tipping back a bottle of Keith's. On the table is his sketch pad and pencil. In the distance is a grinning scar of rich red shoreline. White-tipped breakers rise and curl into question marks before crashing against a ridge of rocks.

It's been a pleasant holiday, tooling around in his beat-up Lada to a succession of historic lighthouses, provincial parks and craft shops. Sketching fishermen harvesting Irish moss on the shore of North Cape. Stuffing himself at a New Glasgow lobster supper. The inevitable tour of Green Gables House in Cavendish. Tomorrow he is supposed to drive back home to Toronto to start a job in an ad agency.

His father had asked, "Why Prince Edward Island?"

Samson merely shrugged. "I've never been there."

He recently graduated from the Ontario College of Art. His parents offered to send him to Amsterdam, thinking he'd like to see a bit of his heritage, in remembrance of his late grandfather. *Zaide* Jakob had lived with them when Samson was a child, later moving into the Maimonides Home for Seniors.

Two girls sit at a far table on the patio. One has red hair; the other's is blue-black. Samson opens the pad to a blank sheet.

When *Zaide* Jakob was still living in the upstairs extra room he used to tell Samson about the Nazi occupation of Amsterdam. The overcrowded cattle cars rattling to the Westerbork transit camp and then on to Auschwitz.

"Couldn't you just run away?"

Sometimes the old man would shrug, "Where could I go?" Or else his eyes lit up wildly: "What, and give those bastards the satisfaction of shooting me?"

The waitress brings milkshakes to the girls' table. They sip, giggling to themselves. Samson draws on his pad, capturing distinctive features in a few strokes. The redhead's upturned nose. The dark one's penetrating eyes.

Every night *Zaide* Jakob told about people being starved and gassed. To Samson these were merely bedtime stories. He was only ever scared when woken up by his grandfather's screams from down the hall. The old man must have given himself nightmares with his own stories.

Samson gives the redheaded girl pigtails and a wide straw hat.

After his grandfather died, Samson ate little and spent days in bed. His parents were worried that he might not graduate. Samson didn't care one way or the other.

He quickly sketches a Star of David armband for the dark-haired girl. A sleeve is rolled up to reveal numbers on her forearm. His two misfit Annes stare back at him. One with freckles around her nose, the other with shadows under her eyes. Each girl's hand clasping the other's. Unwilling to let go.

"Where can any of us go?" He says this to himself.

A wave crashes against the distant rocks. Samson breathes deeply, slipping into a world reduced to salt and light. The water recedes, then swells once more. He feels his grandfather's wild eyes blazing inside his brain.

New Glasgow Kiss

There's no one to meet Gregor MacEwan when his plane lands at the Charlottetown Airport. He breathes a sigh of relief, followed by a pinprick of disappointment. He is also taken aback by the airport's smallness and distinct lack of crowd and bustle, bringing to mind a great empty waiting room. There's only a handful of other travellers in the whole place. It is a full ten minutes before his suitcase shows up, inching its way along on the conveyor belt.

Before he left Scotland he had written to Rena a number of times. He'd had no expectations of receiving a reply from her and was not disappointed when it became painfully obvious that one was not forthcoming. In fact, it was more likely that Rena had tossed his letters straight into the bin unopened.

All during the flight from Glasgow to Halifax he had fretted over the thought of her showing up—one minute wishing it would happen, the next praying she wouldn't be there. His fretting was compounded by not being able to smoke on the plane. He kept feeling the patch under the sleeve of his cotton shirt. That miracle of modern science was just the thing for satisfying his craving for nicotine. Closing his eyes, he imagined he could feel the circle of adhesive material pumping the drug through his pores and into his bloodstream. But a patch was no substitute for the oral soothing of a proper fag, especially when something was agitating his soul. He had considered nipping to the toilet for a quick puff, but decided it wasn't worth the bother it could bring. In the end he made do with the extra packet of pretzels he had palmed off the pretty blonde flight attendant's tray.

In Halifax there'd been a forty-five-minute layover before the cramped Air Nova twenty-seater took off for Charlottetown. He found the only designated smoking area: a secluded bench near a Dumpster outside of the airport. Fetching a packet of Golden Virginia and some Rizla papers from his flight bag, he rolled himself a desperately needed smoke and lit up. After his fag, he repaired to a suitably dim bar called Legends, and ordered a beer to chase the whiskeys he'd had in flight.

Gregor hadn't seen or spoken to Rena for over six years, not since she left Glasgow after Magda died. She had sworn never to return. He knew she still blamed him for Magda's death.

After he'd been released from prison, he managed to discover through friends of hers that she had lived in different parts of Canada. Toronto, Ottawa, Montreal. A little more detective work put her last place of residence as somewhere in the tiny province of Prince Edward Island. He couldn't help grinning when he finally tracked down an address for her. A town called, of all things, New Glasgow.

By the time he came into possession of this vital piece of information, more than a year had passed since his release, during which he worked a string of odd jobs and saved a good bit of *dosh*. He knew he would have to apply for a passport to travel out of the country and had little hope of obtaining one, due to his prison record. The whole point of wanting to reconcile with his estranged daughter was to steer himself onto a new road. The straight and narrow, as it's always called. But life's queer that way. In order to put himself in that direction, he called in one last favour from a mate who knew someone who had a cousin who was something of an artist when it came to forging official documents. It took a good chunk out of his savings, but in less than a month he was holding a perfectly crafted Scottish passport, issued to one *Gregory McEuen*. Much to his surprise, the altered spelling of his name allowed him to pass through Canada Customs without any problem.

It's a bright May afternoon as he steers his rented Chrysler along the twisting roller coaster of roadway, passing wooded hills and a countryside slowly turning leafy green. There are still patches of snow covering the brown grass. He rolls the window down and inhales a brisk slice of spring into his lungs. He'd had a hunch New Glasgow would be different from the original. Aside from the nagging strangeness of driving on the wrong side of the road—something he knows he could never get used to—he's feeling well chuffed by all this bucolic splendour.

Gregor parks at the address on New London Road, which he had found on a pamphlet at the tourist kiosk in the airport. It's a picturesque clapboard house, the earthy colour of mustard seed with rust red trimming. The same rich shade as the red soil he's been seeing everywhere. Even from the plane it had caught his eye. A good honest colour.

The house has a pleasingly simple, rough-hewn charm to it, with the glaring exception of the grey satellite dish jutting from the side of the roof. Gregor steps up to the wooden porch and knocks at the front door. A stout woman in a purple track suit answers.

"'Scuse me," he says. "The name's MacEwan. I belled you from the airport about the room. Are ye Mrs. Gallant?"

"I am." She recognizes the gravel-edged accent. Obviously from away. She makes a slow appraisal of this tall, burly man with the blunt chin, flinty eyes and thinning ginger hair. "Come in. Can I make you a cuppa tea?"

Inside there's a cozy sitting room, featuring a stone-built fireplace draped with fishing net and seashells. He follows Mrs. Gallant through a narrow vestibule, adorned with delicate watercolours of maritime scenes. Passing a small den, he notices a treadmill machine with a TV in front of it.

"I didnae know you had a wee gym in the place," he says jovially. "I should've brought ma trainers along."

Finally, they enter a large yellow kitchen. A kettle whistles on a modern gas range. In the opposite corner is a smaller and older wood stove with a fire blazing inside. Gregor warms his hands over the black iron top. Mrs. Gallant swirls hot water in a porcelain teapot, pours it out, then drops in three bags and fills the pot with steaming water. Beckoning him to sit at the wide table, she sets out cups, saucers, spoons, milk jug and sugar bowl.

"So. How long do you expect to be home?" she asks.

"Home?"

"On the Island. We don't really get tourists 'til later in the summer."

"Aye. Tae be honest, I'm kinda here on some personal business and I don't know how long it'll take."

She pours their tea and pulls a chair near to him. Despite his casual manner he sits rigidly and holds the cup carefully in both hands.

"That tattoo's some stark looking, if you don't mind me saying," she says, referring to the dark blue letters on his left hand, just above the scarred knuckles, that spell MAGDA. "A girlfriend?"

"Nae. Me wife. Passed on now."

"I'm sorry. My husband is also dead. Died while he was in prison. Pneumonia."

Gregor fidgets in his seat. "Sorry for your loss."

"That was some few years back. The first time I visited him at the Dorchester Pen I saw he had a tattoo. Did it himself with a sewing needle and shoe polish. Only it said Chantal and my name is Grace."

"Oh." Feeling uneasy, he tries to think of a way to steer the subject away from prison.

"The thing is ..." she continues, regarding him, not unkindly, through her bifocals. "His tattoo was much like yours. I'm guessing yours was made under ... um, similar circumstances, shall we say?"

"That's me sussed," he says with a nervous laugh. He starts to trace the M on his hand with the tip of his finger and stops, thinking it looks like he's trying to rub it off.

"Please don't be upset," says Mrs. Gallant. "I don't mean to judge. It's just I like to know who's staying in my house. Can't be too careful you know."

"I cannae deny it. It's true I've done a stretch."

"What for?"

"Possession of stolen goods. And assault. I gave a cop a Glasgow kiss."

"A what?"

"When he was nabbing me I stuck the *heid* in him." He jerks his head forward, demonstrating a vicious head butt. Mrs. Gallant winces. "Aye, both our melons were *loupin'* hard after that. But I had a long time to get over mine. I got five years in the Bar L."

"The barrel?"

"Barlinnie. Believe me, five years there is worth double the time anywhere else. I been out now a bit more than a year. Tryin' tae start over like."

He looks out the window; the sky is clear as a watercolour. "See, my daughter lives here. Her name is Rena. I don't know if she goes under MacEwan anymore. She might be Weitz. That was my wife's name. Do you know of her?"

"Rena? You must mean Dr. Choudhury's wife. I believe that's her name. She has a Scottish accent."

"Married, is she? To a doctor an' all. We haven't kept in touch much. I'm no even sure she knows I'm here."

Mrs. Gallant stares into her empty cup, as if searching for something. "Well," she finally says. "The room is fifty dollars a day. Three hundred and twenty-five for the week. Breakfast included."

"The week will be fine." He pulls out his wallet. "I'd be happy tae pay ye in advance, if that's your preference."

"That's not necessary, Mr. MacEwan. I'm a pretty good judge of character."

"More'n that," he says, slurping back the dregs of his tea. "You'd make a brilliant detective. And by the way, Mr. MacEwan was ma da's name. I prefer tae be called Gregor."

As a joke, Magda used to call him Gregor Samsa, after the character in the Franz Kafka story, *Metamorphosis*. When she told him it was about a man who woke up to find himself turned into an insect, he figured she was just trying to wind him up, because she loved to read and he had no use for books. She had come from a middle-class family of Jewish Czech immigrants who owned a newsagent in Shawlands. Gregor himself grew up in a grey council flat in Govan. When sober, his father worked on and off as a carpenter in the shipyards and his mother died of tuberculosis when Gregor was eight.

While in Barlinnie, Gregor tried to find some peace and quiet in the library and discovered a collection of Kafka's stories. He read *Metamorphosis*. It was a revelation. This was a story about Gregor's own experience, what it was like to wake up in a tiny cell every day. No matter where he was—the mess hall, the laundry room, the exercise yard—he had felt as insignificant and trapped as an insect, unable to turn this way or that, just like that poor bastard in the story.

Magda had been right. He was Gregor Samsa. It was too funny. And painful, because it made him miss her even more. He felt grateful to her. More than just winding him up, she had given him a way to do his time, to make it bearable somehow. The trick was to become an insect, blending into the woodwork with a bloody-minded instinct for survival. He tore the story out of the book and kept the pages under his pillow. Then, with a razor blade and ink from a ballpoint pen, he immortalized his darling dead wife's name on his hand.

Early the next morning Gregor stands on a bridge with the collar of his leather jacket turned up, shoulders hunched and hands pushed into pockets. He watches remnants of ice drifting on the Clyde. The cold air brings tears to the corners of his red-lidded eyes. Despite the cloud-like mattress and heavy down-filled comforter in Mrs. Gallant's guestroom, he had slept fitfully.

He's smoking his fifth cigarette this morning. His tongue feels raw and bitter. He has no appetite. Even the aroma of Mrs Gallant's freshly baked rolls had failed to tempt him. He barely gulped down a cup of tea before leaving the house.

He walks on the flat, dewy grass by the road. Only a car and a pickup truck have passed him so far. The sun is starting to glare over the tops of trees. He sees the modern white bungalow with the blue roof. It's perched on a hill surrounded by pines, just as Mrs. Gallant had described it. By the road is a mailbox that says THE CHOUDHURYS.

He knows he should have called first. Mrs. Gallant had offered the use of her telephone. A couple of times he had picked up the receiver and immediately put it back in its cradle.

The mailbox is at the foot of a black paved driveway that curves up the hill to a large garage with two doors. One of the doors opens and Gregor moves behind a fat birch tree. A jeep drives out and the door automatically starts to close behind it. He gets a glimpse of the driver. A dark-skinned man. Once the jeep reaches the road, it speeds off in the direction away from him. Gregor notices the garage door only closes halfway.

Then a yellow school bus lumbers up the road and stops at the foot of the driveway. The front door of the bungalow opens and a young dark-skinned boy wearing a knapsack runs down the driveway. He climbs into the bus, which immediately motors off.

It doesn't register at first and he wonders if he has the wrong place. Why are dark-skinned people coming out of Rena's house? Of course. Choudhury. He'd never reckoned that his daughter married an Indian. Not to mention giving birth to a dusky *wean*. His grandson.

Gregor walks up the driveway, stopping at the garage. He ducks his head under the partially closed door and steps in. There is a station wagon parked inside. She must be home. *Either go ring the bloody doorbell or leave*, he chides himself.

Instead, without thinking, he opens the passenger door of the station wagon. The light inside the car turns on. He half-expects to hear an alarm, but there's nothing. On the passenger seat is a folded piece of paper that looks familiar. Picking it up, he sees it's the last letter he had written to her. All the information is here, when he was arriving, his hope of patching things up between them. He had found more comfort believing she'd thrown out his letters without opening them. Maybe then he'd have a chance. But here was the proof that she wanted nothing to do with him. She didn't write back. Wouldn't even meet his plane.

He suddenly feels like a thief. A weird feeling of déjà vu. So many times during some job—breaking into a warehouse or ripping off a lorry—he had his little girl's face floating in his head. Her look of disappointment, of anger and worry. Funny how it never stopped him from doing the crime. In a way, seeing her face in his head had let him focus on the job. Like having a disapproving guardian angel hovering over his shoulder.

Rena's attitude toward him worsened after Magda went into hospital. Cancer of the brain. The doctors told them it was only a matter of time. Rena was twenty then. Had her first proper job in an insurance office. All grown up and responsible. They took shifts with Magda, him sitting with her during the day and Rena coming in the evening after work. That way they missed running into each other and he could avoid her condemnation.

The night Magda died he'd been arrested with a van full of hot VCRs. After that Rena's disapproval of him hardened into cold disgust.

Holding the letter and knowing she ignored it brings back the full force of that disgust, worse than a kick in the stomach or a head butt. With those you're in pain but you know you're there. Now he feels like a ghost. Like being back in Barlinnie. Back at square one. An insect unable to move this way or that, knowing he'll never be able to make any progress at all.

He puts the letter back on the passenger seat, closes the car door and hurries down the driveway to the road.

But you came such a long way.

Mrs. Gallant's words echo in his ears as he turns onto the parking lot of the Charlottetown Airport. She's a good woman. Did her best to talk him into at least staying out the week. But he doesn't see the point. It was a mistake to come in the first place. It cost him a few quid, but if all we ever pay in this life is money we're getting off cheap. Oddly enough, it was Magda's father who had said that to him. Right before he gave Gregor fifty pounds to stay away from his daughter. Gregor threw it back in his face. Maybe he should've listened.

The airport looks bigger than he remembers. Emptier. Lonelier. He carries his bags toward the ticket counter. From the corner of his eye he sees someone approaching, but pays no mind. All at once the person is actually blocking his way. Some woman. A cloud of annoyance furrows his brow until he looks her in the face.

Rena.

Something cold runs through him and he realizes he couldn't move even if she wasn't in his way. She really hasn't changed that much. He'd know his own daughter anywhere. Still, it's a total stranger standing before him.

"Comin' tae see me off then?" he manages to say without betraying the catch in his throat.

"I didn't know you were rollin' in the *poppy* that you can afford day excursions to Canada." Through narrowed eyes she tries to take in the whole image of him.

"How did you know I was here?"

"A wee birdie."

"You mean Mrs. Gallant stickin' her nose in."

"Never mind that," says Rena. "I heard you was prowlin' around in my garage."

"I wanted tae ring ... but I just lost ma nerve." He is aware of how tightly he's gripping his suitcase and puts it down, but leaves the flight bag slung around his shoulder.

"So you came sneakin' round instead. Bloody typical."

His face, up until now a stiff grey mask of contrition, suddenly flares red and splinters into deep lines of anguish. "What else could I do? You never bloody wrote me back."

"I didn't know what tae write, did I? I figured if I didn't write at all you wouldn't come."

He says nothing and reaches down for his suitcase. It's then that Rena notices the crude tattoo on his hand: her mother's name.

"A souvenir from prison, is it?" she says, the quaver in her voice spreading throughout her tiny frame. "Keeping her alive through self-mutilation. Taking the *pish* out of her misery. Or is that from guilt, then. A thief's penance?"

As if acting on an impulse of its own, the tattooed hand stops short of the suitcase and shoots up, slapping his daughter square on the side of the face. In horror, he watches her reel backward as the sound—a sickening sharp crack—echoes in the pit of his stomach. He reaches out to keep her from falling, but she has regained her balance and raises her thin arms to protect herself.

The airport personnel are watching now and Gregor steps back. "God strike me dead."

He looks around but there's a fog billowing behind his eyes. He is distracted by the glare of sunshine off the glass exit doors and hastens in their direction, stumbling toward the escape route from a bad dream. He hears a voice—so far away now—calling to him as the glass doors slide open and he rushes into the bright afternoon, nearly knocking over a backpacking teenage girl.

Once in the parking lot he stops, gulping air into his lungs like one pulled from the brink of drowning. Squinting against the overhead whiteness of the sun, the full shame of his offence—striking his only child—burning into his face.

So is that what this was all about, coming all this way? Just to drive the last nail into the coffin? A permanent wedge that would do what no ocean could? Never in his whole life had he raised a hand to her. He'd cut the bloody thing off right here and now before he'd do it again. He stares at the tattoo of his dead wife's name, the letters looking like spidery blue veins, the lifeblood of her memory coursing through them. All he wanted was this living connection again. So how could he come this far only to fail so quickly?

"Here."

Rena sets his suitcase on the asphalt between them. Then without another word she turns and walks toward the row of cars at the back end of the parking lot, getting into the driver's side of a tan station wagon. Gregor recognizes it as the one he'd seen in her garage. It's obviously an older model but looks new out in the full flush of daylight. He wonders if it's been washed since yesterday and then feels stupid for thinking it. He watches, waiting for the engine to start, but after a few minutes the car is still sitting there silently.

He considers leaving the suitcase where it is, then bends wearily to pick it up and walks over to the station wagon. The passenger's door is locked so he sets his suitcase and flight bag down and goes around to the driver's side. Her door is also locked and the window is up, despite the sun beating against the windshield, which must be making the inside hot and stuffy. Both of her hands are gripping the top of the steering wheel and she stares straight ahead. Gregor taps her window lightly with a red, calloused knuckle, making sure he uses his right hand, the one that's not tattooed.

"I cannae see how we can have a conversation with a pane of glass between us."

The window rolls down a crack. "Your flight leaves in half an hour. You should probably check in." She continues staring ahead.

"It's an open ticket."

The last time they had seen each other was at Magda's funeral, a few days after his arraignment. He'd been remanded with no bail because he was deemed a flight risk and dangerous because he had attacked one of the arresting officers. The *Glasgow kiss* had caused a large purple welt to form at the peak of his hairline, where he'd smashed his head down on the policeman's.

In the Cathcart Hebrew Cemetery, with hands cuffed behind his back, he was accompanied by three plainclothesmen and received murderous stares from his in-laws, not to mention the occasional nervous glance from the rabbi. Rena could hardly bring herself to look at him. Instead, she focused her rage toward the hole in the ground, into which the casket was being lowered.

The one brief moment when their eyes did meet it was obvious the purple welt shocked her. She'd quickly averted her eyes, but a torrent of tears streamed down her wan cheeks. Gregor felt guilty, but he also felt the faintest sense of having fulfilled a familial duty by being the catalyst of his daughter's show of unbridled grief. But only the catalyst. He didn't dare entertain the delusion that his daughter was crying for anything other than the loss of the woman who had brought her into this world.

As is the Jewish custom, the family members had begun to take turns shovelling earth into the grave. When the shovel was passed to Rena, rather than tossing in the obligatory mound of dirt, she started to work in earnest, heaving one shovelful of earth after the other. Working out all her grief and fury in good honest work, unlike her old man. Even from the distance where he stood, Gregor could see the sheen of sweat on her brow as she put her shoulder into the physical labour. She showed no signs of letting up as the plainclothesmen led him back to their unmarked car.

The day has grown warmer. He takes off his coat and slings it over his shoulder, feeling the wetness circling the armpits of his cotton shirt. Gregor notices Rena's station wagon has been soiled by a white blob of bird shit right on the metal trim where the roof and windshield meet. He contemplates cleaning it off, but remembers how Magda had told him that having a bird shit on you is a Jewish omen for *mazel* or good luck. As usual, he'd reckoned she was just winding him up.

All at once her absence opens a windless space inside him. He feels the sun's rays penetrating the space, the way they would just above the walls of the exercise yard in Barlinnie.

"I hear you married a doctor."

Rena looks up at him with a distrusting squint. "That's right."

"What's his name?"

"Ashok."

"Aye?" He could feel her eyes drilling into him. "And the lad?"

"Michael, but everyone calls him Mikey."

"An English name then?"

"I named him for my mother," she says, referring to the Jewish tradition of naming a child with the same initial as a dead relative. "His middle name is Naresh. It means *king*."

"And how does he get on at school?" Gregor asked with genuine interest.

"He's very bright."

"I've no doubt of that. I mean how does he get on with his classmates, and in this small community, with a dark father and a white mother?"

Her mouth purses into a rigid bud, but her eyes flare up with self-satisfaction, knowing it would come to this. "Mikey gets on just fine. His father happens tae be the family doctor for many people in New Glasgow. He's a respected member of the community. It's a small place, but most everyone is broad-minded. Not like some."

Gregor shakes his head. "I was no tryin' tae judge. I've nothing against a person's skin. Surely, you know that. I'm a lot of things but I'm no prejudiced."

She rolls her eyes and stares at the dashboard, biting the inside of her lip, breathing steadily though her nose like she's afraid to open her mouth.

"Give us a break," he says. "I'm just concerned about ma ain grandson. I've a right to that, surely. I mean, up until yesterday I didn't even know I had one."

She turns on him, eyes ablaze. "Don't act it with me! You've no right to be here giving me *gyp*. Fuck off back to where you came from."

"Look, Rena, we're getting nowhere like this. How can we have a proper talk with this window between us? It's like visiting day in Barlinnie."

"I can only imagine the visitors you had."

"You sure as hell weren't one of 'em," he says bitterly. "You *shot the craw* as soon as your mother was buried."

"I *shot the craw* to get *shot* of you and the life that killed my mother. I couldn't put it behind me fast enough."

"I won't make excuses for my bad ways. But you cannae blame me for your mother's death."

He's bending down now, speaking directly into the crack of the open window. There's a curiously savage look on his daughter's face as she flips up the door lock. Before he can move away the door swings open with a terrible force, the top of it smashing against his forehead. Gregor reels backwards, sprawling against the side of the car parked in the next space, then crumples to his knees on the hot asphalt. Rena is standing over him.

"Then who do I bloody well blame if not you? Where were you the night she died?"

He starts to open his mouth, but Rena's not waiting for an answer.

"Where were you while I was sitting there, listening to her barely getting her words out? Begging me to help her. Where were you when she squeezed my hand with what was left of her strength?"

Gregor tries to get to his feet, but can't quite manage it. He looks to Rena, but she makes no move. Her hands are balled into white trembling fists. Her thin red face is wet with tears, the mouth twisted and baring teeth.

"Where the fuck were you when I didn't know what else to do? When I couldn't bear it anymore? You weren't there to see the look of relief in her eyes before I covered her with the pillow. When I pushed down with all my weight and felt her struggling. You weren't there to help her. You selfish bastard." She passes her sleeve across her wet eyes. The skin sags wearily below bladed cheekbones. "You should've been there to stop me."

Gregor stares up at his daughter. A moment earlier she seemed to take up the whole sky, like a great ball of flame. But now she is thin, wavering, a wisp of smoke curling up toward the clouds before disappearing altogether. He wants to extend his hand out to her, but finds it leaden and useless on the asphalt. She folds herself back into the station wagon. Gregor can only watch in mute suffering as the automobile backs out of the parking space, turns and drives off toward the exit.

When he finally rises unsteadily to his feet, a slight dizziness turns the parking lot into a tilt-a-whirl ride. Taking a moment to find his bearings, he gathers up his bags. At first he heads in the direction of the airport's glass doors, but changes his mind when he notices his rented Chrysler. It hasn't been picked up yet. He hobbles over to it, tosses his bags into the back seat, opens the front door and collapses behind the wheel. The keys are still lodged inside the driver's sunshade, where he'd left them. There's still enough time to check his bags and board the plane. Instead, he rolls a smoke.

He studies his forehead in the rear-view mirror. Nice red mark there. She must have put her whole weight into smashing that door into him. In a day or two it should start to turn a yellowish purple.

He tries to picture it in his mind, her standing over Magda, pillow in her hands, poised in mid-air. Some hidden welt inside him starts to burn and throb, changing from dumbfounded red to self-pitying yellow, from murderous purple to bottomless black.

He finishes his fag and rolls another one, feeling like he could sit in this parking lot for the rest of his life. Probably should go to a hospital to have his head looked at. But what he really needs right now is a whiskey.

Above the airport's roof, the Air Nova jet he is supposed to be on ascends toward Halifax. He sticks his head out the window to watch it shrink in the distance, getting smaller and smaller, but not yet out of sight.

Phone Booth

It's pissing miserably when I duck into a phone booth across the street from your building. The rain is drumming against the glass with a thousand nervous fingers. I push the dripping hair out of my eyes. Water oozing down the gutters behind my ears. My shirt and jeans are plastered to me. A thick membrane. I clench my toes and the sickening squelch shoots directly to the pit of my stomach.

Please be home, Lisa.

I dig out a quarter from my pocket and push it into the slot. Punching your number, counting the rings, my heart bobs on choppy waters of hope and despair. It's the machine and your voice telling me you can't come to the phone right now but if I leave a message you promise to call right back. I want to believe the voice, but quickly hang up when I hear the beep.

Why, Lisa? Why can't you come to the phone right now? What are you doing up there? Who's with you?

Maybe you really aren't home yet. Maybe if I wait long enough I'll see you coming in. I'll wait all night if I have to. Water seeps between the plastic partitions. Wild rivulets down the glass flare up from passing headlights. Any one of them could be you.

The heavens empty, washing down all the concrete and steel, cutting through all that smudged graffiti and garbage, all that dog shit and smoke and dust—sluicing the whole mess down through the sewer grates.

And when the city is clean and new, Lisa, and all the past misunderstandings have been cleared away, then will you believe me? Would that make you understand how much I love you? It's wrong for us not to be together.

The moment I first saw you I knew we were meant to be together. The way you stood alone at the party, your long brown hair practically covering your face, trying to blend in with the wall. What drew me was the way you were there and not there, fading in and out like a shaky radio wave. I felt like a satellite being pulled toward you. It's different for me. I always feel too present in the world. There's no way of escaping. You looked at me with this shy expression, about to turn away, but we were already dancing and I held you tight in case you started fading out again. Hoping you would take me with you so I wouldn't feel the world so much. Then I felt you holding me too. Pressing into me, your body pleading with me to deliver you into the world. I knew then that you and I could balance each other out. I still know it and I'll always believe it. We're two halves of a whole, fated to fit together.

Those first moments, Lisa, they were the purest I've ever experienced. Such a delicate balance between us. If only we could have kept on dancing and never stopped. I know I did some things that were bad. I couldn't help myself. It's because I'm in the world too much. I feel like Atlas and it's all pushing down on my shoulders. All of it trying to crush me. Me alone. Please, Lisa, I can't be alone. You can't shut me out this way. I won't let you.

There's a sudden boom of thunder. The booth rattles violently. The rain is a dazzling wall. I can barely see the front door of your building. What if I miss you? What if you never know that I've been waiting here?

I slam another coin into the slot and punch the numbers again. This time I can hear the lie in that sweet innocent message. *Call right back* my ass. I've been discarded along with everything else. Another chalk smudge running down some forgotten wall, another turd pummelled into the sidewalk crack. Flushed away and forgotten. You can't do that to me. Nobody does that to me.

When the beep comes I don't hang up, but something seizes inside my throat so I push my arm through the partitions. The metal cord is taut and vibrating as I hold the receiver outside. Listen to the unstoppable torrent hammering the pavement's gleaming indifference. You need to know the terrible truth of thunder cracking the sky in two, the cruel rumbling of a world crashing down on itself. You can try all you like to shield yourself from my reasoning, my arguments, my pleading. Words are useless now. I let the elements do my talking. This is me speaking in my true voice.

When I hang up the phone, a moment of satisfaction swells inside me like an ever-expanding universe of planets and stars continuously brightening and burning. Then everything slowly blurs into disappointment. Who am I kidding? To you the message will be just static and noise. You'll probably erase it without a second thought. I become aware of how narrow this phone booth really is. A coffin. Or is it a womb? All my hopes stillborn. I can imagine you shaking your head in pity.

Don't try to fool me into thinking that you pity me, Lisa. Letting the rain do your crying for you, pretending to muster up an ounce of sympathy for me.

What little I have I'd give to you, but I know it's not enough. You ask for clear skies and sunshine, for the cool dew of morning and a night full of glittering stars. But the in-between times, all those stormy moments that make up who I am, they scare you with their demands on your patience and understanding, courage and desire, of having to give something of yourself. It's easy for you, Lisa. You move so effortlessly in and out of the world. Whenever things aren't going right you just disappear, fading into the background. I know you keep thinking someone better will come along. Someone who can keep you safe, who won't ask too much of you. I want to give you everything, Lisa, but I can only offer my passion in all its sudden and unpredictable forms.

Now that I think of it, maybe the real problem is that I have too much to give and you want so little. I hear the rain now and it doesn't sound like anything at all. That endless hissing is just the slow erosion of everything I thought we could be to each other.

Across the street a cab pulls up to your building. I try to rush out of the phone booth, but half way through I'm wedged hopelessly between the partitions. I can see you walking up the front steps of your building. I yell your name but you don't hear me. I'm banging madly on the side of the phone booth, struggling to push myself through. One last lunge and I explode onto the sidewalk.

Lisa! Lisa! I just want one minute, that's all I want.

You see it's me. I know you can hear me. Why do you have to turn away like I don't exist? If you can't see me I'll disappear? So I grabbed you that one time. Because you were fading away, trying to tune me out. I didn't mean to hurt you. I wanted to pull you back into the world. I wanted to be an anchor for you. The same way I took you in my arms when we danced together, perfectly balanced. But this one time I kept shaking you. I couldn't help it. You weren't listening, not even trying to understand my side of things. How I can't stop thinking about you. How no one else will ever be able to make you happy. Because you're a stuck-up bitch who'll be alone for the rest of your life. No one will want you. Only me.

Here's the deal, Lisa. I'll stay on the sidewalk and you stand up there by the door.

Go ahead and call for the police. There wasn't much they could do last time. They know this is something we have to work out on our own. Now you're scrambling through your purse, but I've come too far, waited too long. I pull the gun from the back of my jeans before you can take the key out and unlock the door.

It all happens at once. The sound of the shot—the ripping burn in my temple and that helpless domino sense of falling backwards. The whole world reeling back on its axis. Street lamps and cars and lit-up signs tumble over themselves. The world through the round window of a washing machine. Everything is that small, that meaningless. The jumble we're always sorting through, trying to create some kind of order. Trying to impose our will onto the dark whorl of chaos.

I feel myself sprawled across the sidewalk. My head hanging backward over the curb. The rushing gutter in my hair. Across the street I can see the upside-down phone booth suspended over Heaven's bottomless pit.

I can hear you, Lisa, your voice like a broken record: *Why? Why? Why?*

Who cares? Nothing matters anymore. You're dead to me now.

Elephant Rock

Winter has finally butchered Elephant Rock, the trunk eroded away entirely. Now it's a thick, reddish formation rising up from the craggy shoreline of North Cape, with the white salivating waves of the Northumberland Strait lashing at all sides.

It's the first day of spring. Under a pale sky Nancy and Raj stand behind the flimsy chain-link fence near the edge of the cliff to look down at the monolithic rock. The flat top, still covered with snow, is showing grassy brown patches.

"I've lived on PEI all my life and this is the first time I've ever been here," says Nancy. "Elephant Rock is this really famous landmark and I never saw it before today."

"My parents took me here when we first moved from Goa," says Raj. "I was twelve. The trunk was still attached then. They saw it as being a good omen, an elephant in our new home."

Raj has just turned eighteen. Nancy is a few months older. They'll both graduate this summer; he from Colonel Gray senior high and she from the Rural. They met almost a year ago at the Charlottetown

Farmer's Market, where Raj sometimes helps out at his mother's stall, serving *chapatis* and *samosas*. Nancy works at the next stall over, which is the juice bar, on Saturdays.

In the fall Raj plans to go into Business Administration at UPEI, but Nancy has been accepted to Concordia University in Montreal to study languages. They've made the two-hour drive to North Cape in the used Dodge Neon her parents bought her for graduation.

"I really should be home studying," says Nancy. The wind whips her orange hair into a jittery flame and flaps the vents of her canvas coat. The chain-link fence rattles like chattering metal teeth.

"You can study tonight."

Raj's jean jacket is buttoned right to the top with the collar flipped up. He warms Nancy's slender hands by sandwiching them between his own.

"I'm not leaving until August," she says. "We still have time."

Raj fishes something from the pocket of his jean jacket—a ring, thin and silver, with the fiery eye of a ruby set in the middle—and slips it on Nancy's finger.

"My grandmother left it to me after she died. I want you to have it."

Nancy raises her hand. The ruby seems to glitter with a cold anger.

"It's beautiful, but your parents …"

"The ring is mine," Raj says impatiently. "I can do what I want with it."

A sudden gust snaps the chain-link fence in two, leaving nothing between them and the edge of the cliff. Raj instinctively pulls Nancy to him. They're both mesmerized by the fine line between solid ground and thin air. Nancy hugs Raj's neck, her mouth close to his ear.

"I've been waiting all my life to get off this island," she says under her breath.

"I will always be *from away*," he answers. "And yet, here I am." He can't help feeling he has let her down.

Elephant Rock is not what it was. The trunk finally eroded away. For Nancy and Raj the very air around them seems charged by that moment of butchery and rebirth, leaving only this incarnation of solitude that rises from the frenzied dance of the waves below.

The Same Machine

The spliff burns down to a glowing red o of cardboard filter. Del sucks deep and explodes into raw jagged coughing. His twig-thin body doubles over and for a minute I think he might snap in two. So many times, whenever it was me hacking up my guts after a harsh toke, Del would slap me hard on the back and say: "One of these days the two of us'll end up in the hospital hooked up to the same machine."

I've always imagined some huge iron lung with both of us attached by a tangle of tubes and wires.

It's on the tip of my tongue to say it back to him. But things are different now. Del passes the roach to me. There's nothing left and I flick it into the fireplace.

"Got a nice buzz off that," I say, lighting up a smoke. "You?"

"Not bad." He's rasping, gulping back air. "Takes a bit of the edge off anyway."

It was Del's idea for us to drive to my cottage after his chemo. The plan was that I'd be waiting in my van in the Royal Vic's parking lot with a doob rolled and ready to be fired up. I was sure I had an ounce stashed under some laundry in my apartment on St. Urbain. I turned the whole place upside down before remembering it was still sitting in my freezer behind some frozen Michelina's dinners and a bottle of Stoli back in North Hatley. I felt shitty for letting Del down like that. To make up for it, I swerved in and out of the Friday afternoon Montreal traffic and put the pedal to the metal all the way east along the Autoroute. I kept glancing over at Del slumped down in the seat. He was staring ahead at the windshield like he was looking for his reflection in a blank mirror.

Now we're here in my cottage in North Hatley and he's lying on my beat-up futon sofa, partly covered with a plaid, wool blanket and propping himself up against a couple of pillows. I toss the last of the wood on the fire.

"It's cold out here in the evening. I should've ordered another cord."

"Don't worry," he says.

"You need another blanket?"

"I'm good."

"Hang on, I know." I go to the kitchen and come back to the living room with the bottle of Stoli and a couple of glasses. "This'll do the trick."

"Just a small one," he says.

I measure out a half-inch and hand him the glass. I decide to be a little more generous with myself.

"I might have some tomato juice around if you want."

Del shakes his head.

I tap his glass with my own. "Cheers, buddy."

We both toss back our vodkas. I'm savouring the warmth in the pit of my stomach. Del is taking quick breaths and sputters a bit. I'm worried that he'll start choking again. Except for a couple of nasty hacks and some wheezing, he seems to have things under control. His forced grin tries to assure me that it's all good.

"Again?" I hold out the bottle.

"Maybe later."

I pour myself one, knock it back and start rolling another joint. Usually it would be Del doing all the rolling and playing bartender.

The Same Machine

One of his favourite things was to roll up maybe ten to fifteen joints the size of toothpicks and tape them onto random playing cards, then deal Black Jack to me. If he turned up a card with a joint it automatically meant I was over. Dealer wins. Of course we'd have to blow the stick before going on with the game.

These days Del finds it hard to roll. He says he can feel the leukemia worming into his joints, eating away at his bones. I sense his eyes studying how I fold over part of the rolling paper and crease it to form a groove. Then I carefully spread the dope along the groove. I don't dare look up, but I can imagine his eyes as two intense black holes. Tiny camera lenses watching and recording everything.

I do everything slowly, meticulously picking out little bits of lumber and the odd seed. Working the paper gently between my thumbs and fingers, then neatly slipping the lip underneath until it catches. I roll it firm but not too tight. Del hates it when a joint is so tight that it's like sucking cement through a straw and makes your cheeks ache.

I lick the gummed part of the paper, roll it up, then twist one end and use a match to tamp down the loose dope in the other end. Half of the matchbook cover is missing from having strips torn off for filters. Some dudes like to cut the strips with scissors, but Del always took pride in being able to tear it off evenly with his bare fingers. For him it's little things like that that give the whole ritual more meaning. I'm not as good at tearing evenly, one end always being too wide. So I purposely tear micro-inch by micro-inch to make sure everything is perfect.

"I love watching you do that," says Del.

"The anticipation, eh?"

"The luxury of taking your time. When I watch you roll it's like time itself has come to a stop. Like all the clocks are frozen with anticipation."

"Almost as sweet as the high itself," I say.

After I've rolled up the strip of cardboard and fit it into the end of the joint, I hold it up for Del's approval. He claps his hands slowly in what we'd both like to believe is his usual smart-ass, ironic gesture. The real irony is that we know it's plain fatigue.

I light up—a couple of quick puffs to get it burning—and pass it to Del. His fingers don't want to co-operate this time and I hold the joint up to his mouth. There's a pained look on his face as he tries to hold down the smoke.

"Let me know when you're hungry. I'll nuke a couple of frozen dinners for us."

He exhales in one long rush of breath, petering out at the end, his lips making the noise of a balloon shrivelling into nothing. "Maybe later."

We toke in silence. When it gets near the end I'm careful not to let him have any of the filter and get rid of it in the fireplace.

"Fire's dying down," he says.

There are no more logs or kindling, just a pile of old newspapers in the corner. I roll a whole newspaper into a makeshift log and hold it up to my mouth. "How'dja like a hit off this fatty?"

"Fire it up, *mon*," he says in his best Rastafarian accent.

I toss it onto the dying embers. "Check this out."

I use a metal dustpan to fan the embers with broad even strokes as the fire slowly catches and starts to consume the curling pages. Orange and black nerve-endings sizzle into kinetic patterns—the guts of a control panel. An eerie glow of short-circuiting wires. The ghost in the machine. Then the whole thing turns into a grinning jack-o'-lantern, toothless and hysterical, until the mouth opens wider and wider, breaking its hinges to become a gaping jaw of unimaginable agony. I prod a poker into the ashy craw and sparks fly up the chimney—a flurry of microscopic souls being sucked up Eternity's dark tunnel.

"Weird shit, eh?" I give another poke, but now the charred husk only coughs up bits of black paper. "Should I do another one?"

Del's eyes are wet, rims gleaming, threatening to overflow. The outer corners seem to sag from the weight of moisture.

"You okay?"

I can see he's not so much looking into the fireplace as he is into his own head, trying to follow the inner meshing. Maybe watching it come apart bit by bit.

"What do you need? Another blanket?"

He says something under his breath that reaches me as a faint shudder of wind.

"What?"

"It's not ... working ..." he gasps.

"Give it time."

He leans over the side of the sofa and retches. I instinctively move back, but there's nothing coming up. His spindly arms look like straps on a straitjacket as he wraps them around his gut. It makes me cringe to hear that hollow gagging. I can't help thinking of his poor insides all twisted up. Then he dredges up another round of excruciating sounds from the back of his throat until a thin string of something evil trickles out of his throat and down the side of the sofa. For a minute I feel like I also want to spew. I run to the kitchen for a dishtowel. By the time I'm back he's lying flat on the sofa. The nausea seems to have subsided.

"Sorry." He looks up at me with red rheumy eyes. I nod, but concentrate on wiping off the bile from the sofa. All I can do is bunch up the dishtowel and pitch it into the fireplace.

"You think maybe I should roll up another?" I ask.

Without waiting for an answer I tear a Zig-Zag from the packet, grab a clump of weed from the baggie and try to roll it up. The crude joint gets all twisted and crooked in my trembling fingers until the delicate rice paper rips. My hands won't stop shaking. "Wait. Let me ..."

"Forget it," says Del. "It's not helping anymore."

"How can it not be helping?"

I pour myself a double vodka. It's gone in two gulps but does nothing to steady my hands. Outside the day is turning to dusk. The room is darker except for a brilliant streak of sunlight streaming across the sofa, illuminating Del's face.

"Do you want to go to the hospital? I could drive you back to the city."

He closes his eyes. The intensity of the light drains all the blood from his face, giving his skin a smooth ceramic finish. A mask's peaceful fragility.

"You might be more comfortable in the hospital."

Del opens his eyes. "You're in no condition to drive."

"I've been behind the wheel a lot more wasted than this. Remember when we smoked that chillum of *Sinse* with the PCP?"

Del manages a weak smile, a rattle of laughter. "At that party on the West Island?"

"That's right. Who drove us back downtown at four in the morning?"

"How the hell did we make it back in one piece?"

"Damned if I know," I say. "The side of my van was all scratched up."

"That must've been when you scraped the guard rail."

"I did? I think I also pulled a yoo-ee on somebody's lawn."

"Didn't the cops show up?" asks Del.

"I don't know. All I can remember was the traffic lights and street lamps and neon signs all melting into each other."

"I kept laughing so much my body was aching all over."

"And we were both screaming at the top of our lungs." I'm madly punching my palm at the memory of it. "I thought my rib cage was gonna bust open."

Del wipes his eyes. "We definitely should have died that night."

There's still a faint greenish stain of bile on the sofa. I rub my bare forearms. "It's gonna be colder soon. I should really think about burning something in the fireplace."

"What are you going to do?"

"I don't know." I look around the room, sizing up a wicker rocking chair and a three-legged wooden end table.

"It's not like we're going to freeze to death."

I snap at him without thinking. "I know, I know."

"Chill out, man," he says. "Everything's going to be okay."

"How can you say that? Listen to you."

"Don't freak on me, Petey." Del reaches out, barely able to keep his hand suspended. "Please."

I know I should take his hand, but I just stand there, staring like an idiot, afraid to breathe. The hand is a tattered moth hovering for a moment before it flutters back down on his chest and curls up for good.

"It's okay," he says. "I understand."

But I don't.

I go into the kitchen. There's a round oak table with a bowl of sugar, salt and pepper shakers, a bread knife and the phone book. I upend the table and everything slides off, crashing down on the linoleum floor.

Del calls out from the sofa. "Petey? You alright?"

I search around the kitchen but don't see anything I can use. Then I remember the broom closet. Everything in there is a mess but I manage to clear away a broom, a mop and pail and some cardboard tubing before I find the hatchet. Smaller than what I hoped for, but it'll do the trick.

I go for the legs first, metal biting into wood, spitting out white splinters. There's a momentary release, but no real comfort in the violence of each blow. Whatever it is knotting up inside me feels endless. Eternal.

"Hey! What the hell you doing in there?"

It takes a good twenty minutes or so, probably because the blade is pretty dull, but I finally hack the kitchen table into pieces and carry them into the living room. After I rip up some newspaper and lay the wadded balls out in the fireplace, I put the smaller bits of table on it for kindling and the legs and larger pieces on top of that. Then I light the paper. Once the blaze catches, the glow starts dancing around the room, animating Del's face.

"One of these days ..."

"Yeah," he says. "I know."

I sit back, totally done in, and lean my head on the edge of the sofa beside him. The invisible wires between us throw spidery shadows across the ceiling.

FATTED CALF BLUES

1

The eighteen-wheeler pulled into the parking lot of a truck stop about thirty miles out of Dauphin, Manitoba and found a spot beside a line of other rigs. Mavis Jean Bates opened the passenger door and stepped down from the cab, dragging her duffel bag after her.

"Thanks for the ride," she called up to the driver. "You hear of anyone heading west give me a holler. I'll be around."

"Sure thing." The driver remained in the cab and punched the buttons on a cellular phone.

The sweltering July morning stank of hot rubber and exhaust. Stifling waves of heat warped the air and gave the chrome grilles a liquid brilliance.

Mavis Jean's cowboy hat was tilted back, the wide brim framing the hollow-cheeked, nut-brown parchment of her face. The hard angles of her body poked against her denim shirt and faded Levis, resembling a scarecrow made of coat hangers. She strode across the parking lot, boots crunching over sun-baked pebbles and nodded to a small group of truckers standing around one of the rigs.

"How's it going, boys," she said, setting her duffel bag down. "The name's Mavis Jean Bates. You probably heard of my daddy. Everybody knows my daddy. Everybody knows Two-Gun Billy Bates."

Some of the truckers nodded. "Didn't he used to drive for White Line Express?" one of the older ones asked.

"One and the same."

"Had a stroke, didn't he?" said another whose sagging jowls were covered by stubble the colour of cigarette ash.

"Two in total," said Mavis Jean. "First one took him off the road for good. Second one just pushed him farther into himself."

The truckers all nodded appreciatively. A couple bowed their heads.

"Don't think he could survive a third. By all rights he should be in a nursing home or some such place, but my Aunt Vesta won't hear of it. Just talked to her last week and she says he's looking poorlier than ever. That's why I'm trying to get back home to Drumheller."

"Everything's been at a standstill this weekend," said a younger trucker. He had a thick droopy moustache and a green tank top stretched over the beginnings of a pot-belly. A tattoo of a viper coiled around one of his biceps. "Hopefully we'll know where our next loads are by tonight or tomorrow."

"Give me some time to rest up anyway." Mavis Jean wiped the rolled-up part of her sleeve across her brow. "Man alive. Scorcher today, ain't it."

"Brings out the mosquitoes something bad," said one trucker who took a deep drag on a thin black cigar. The long sleeves of his light cotton shirt were buttoned at the cuffs.

"Heard there was another case of West Nile down in Brandon," said a trucker who wore a green John Deere cap.

"That's why I started smoking these Mexican cigars," the long-sleeved trucker said and waved his cheroot in the air like a magic wand. "I get 'em on the Internet. Heard the smoke is supposed to keep the little bastards away."

"*Pee-yoo*!" John Deere held his nose. "Ain't much that stinkweed won't keep away." Hoots of laughter stirred the torpid air like a circle of crows.

Mavis Jean slung the duffel bag's thick strap over her shoulder. "Think I'll go splash some water on my face. Any you boys get wind of a ride heading to Drumheller be sure to let me know."

"You bet, Mavis Jean," said the trucker in the green tank top and offered a hard thick hand. "The name's Curtis."

She liked the firm grip and the directness of his grey eyes. "Good to know you, Curtis."

The truck stop was a large modern complex made of concrete and glass. She'd been here a couple of times before. Over the glass doors was a sign that read: RED RIVER CAFETERIA. The cafeteria took up half of the complex and the other half was a kind of residence with private rooms and communal showers that were for truckers only. A far cry from the homey little greasy spoons and ramshackle motels she used to stay in when out on the road with Two-Gun Billy.

In front of the complex was a spacious semicircle of manicured lawn surrounded by a foot-high retaining wall, which marked off a smaller parking lot for automobiles. As Mavis Jean approached, she saw a young man sitting on the grass in the shade of a white elm. He wore no shirt, baggy army shorts and high tops. His fair arms, shoulders, chest and face were reddened by the sun. The blue and white bandana wrapped pirate-style around his head kept a carroty mop of hair out of his eyes. He was writing in a small notebook.

"Hey there," called Mavis Jean. "I'm trying to get to Drumheller. Could you help me out?"

"Sorry. I am also looking for a ride."

She frowned and noticed the backpack lying nearby. Dead giveaway.

"I thought you were a trucker coming over to offer me a lift," he said.

She forced a tight smile. "Been here a spell?"

"Since last night." He rolled his head in a circle. "I slept in a chair in the television room upstairs. My neck is still stiff."

"You'll live."

He offered his hand. "My name is Milo."

"Mavis Jean."

She pumped the young man's hand. It was small and slender with white tapering fingers. She reckoned it had kept well away from hard work, as opposed to her own hands, which were wiry and callused from ditch digging, baling, fence mending and whatever other kind of manual labour she could pick up here and there. She felt scorn for the kid's moist and gentle grip. Not at all like Curtis' meaty paw.

"Mind if I get myself a bit of that shade?"

"Not at all." He closed the notebook and slid his pen into the spiral binding.

She set down her duffel bag and sat on the grass with her back against the elm's thick trunk. Out of her shirt pocket she fished a flat pouch of Drum tobacco and a booklet of rolling papers, offering some to Milo. He shook his head, but watched with great interest as she dipped the rolling paper into the tobacco pouch, rolled it part way, licked the gummed end of the paper and finished rolling it—all with one hand.

"Where did you learn to do that?"

"My daddy." She took a disposable lighter from her other pocket. "Used to roll while he was driving. He always kept one hand on the wheel. Never even took his eyes off the road. Two-Gun Billy could roll cigarettes in his sleep."

"Two-Gun Billy. Is he an outlaw or something?"

"Never broke the law in his life." She exhaled a thin jet of smoke. "Bent it a little sometimes." She waited for him to laugh but he just stared blankly at her.

"Naw, he was a trucker. I used to go on hauls with him when I was a kid. High up in his rig. Those were the days, sitting in the catbird seat."

"How did he get a name like that?"

"He was a trick shooter before I was born. He had two pearl-handled six-shooters that he could whirl and twirl faster than a gopher craps dirt. Shoot a fly off a tin can at a hundred yards without touching the can. He performed in fairs for a few years." She paused to study the thin coil of smoke rising from the tip of her cigarette. "Then he became a trucker, went to drive for White Line."

"What happened?"

"He quit after my mama died. She was his partner in the show, his assistant. She wore a fancy outfit, all spangles and fringes, and would hold up things, like a matchstick or a playing card, and he would shoot a hole in the card or light the match. Or she would hold a cigarette in her mouth and he would shoot it facing backward while looking in a mirror."

"Do you mind if I ask how she died?"

Mavis Jean was taken aback, less by the question's boldness than by the formality with which it was asked. He had an oddly polite way of talking.

"She died giving birth to me. Some kind of complication. Two-Gun Billy couldn't face doing the act without her. Hung up his guns for good after that."

Milo nodded sympathetically, then reached over to his backpack and dug a box of raisins from one of the outer pouches. He poured out a handful, popped them all into his mouth and offered the box to Mavis Jean. She shook her head.

"So where you going?"

Milo took a minute to finish chewing and swallowed while pouring more raisins into his hand. "Oyen, Alberta."

"Oh yeah? What's there?"

He popped the second batch of raisins into his mouth and took something from his pocket. "I tore this from a newspaper," he said, still chewing, and handed a piece of newsprint to Mavis Jean. She read it slowly.

Slaughtered Cattle A Mystery

> OYEN, Alta —Residents and authorities are mystified by the discovery of three cattle carcasses yesterday morning in a secluded pasture. The animals were apparently cut open and stripped of all their internal organs and bones. Closer inspection of the carcasses revealed the procedures were performed with surgical precision, using sophisticated instruments.

Police have no particular suspects at the moment, but are not ruling out the possibility that this was a cult-like ritual murder. The precise nature of the slaughters has led some people to speculate that it might be the work of extra-terrestrial visitors.

Brad Hoekstra, owner of the cattle, was quoted as saying, "Whoever it was went to a lot of trouble. We're pretty shaken up over the whole thing."

Mavis Jean gave the piece of newspaper back to Milo. "So what do you expect to see in Oyen? Cow carcasses?"

He gazed at the piece of paper for a moment before returning it into his pocket. "I have been dreaming of them."

She gave him a sidelong look. "'Scuse me?"

"I keep a dream diary." He held up his notebook.

"A what?"

"I have been writing down my dreams in this notebook."

"What for?" she asked.

"It is a good discipline. Strindberg kept a dream diary."

"Whoever he is." She lazily flicked away the butt of her cigarette.

"Dr. Veldt says dreams are useful clues to what is lacking in our lives."

"Who's he? Friend of that string bean fellow?"

He quickly flipped through the notebook until he found what he was looking for, then read aloud: "*Last night I dreamed of the cattle again. I was walking through a dark forest with many branches in my way. I then came to a clearing, which was lit by a giant full moon. All around I could see flat shapes on the ground. On further inspection these shapes turned out to be cattle carcasses. They were flat like rugs because their internal organs and bones had been removed. Even their eyes were gone, leaving only empty sockets. All around the perimeter of the clearing carcasses hung from tree branches. I grew scared and looked for a way out of the clearing, but could find no means of escape. As I rushed around I suddenly tripped and was lying amidst the carcasses. I had a strange sensation, as if I would not be able to get up again. That was when I woke up."*

He closed the notebook and seemed to be doing some kind of breathing exercise, taking in a measured amount of air through his nose, holding it for a couple of seconds, then letting it out steadily through pursed lips.

"You okay?"

"Remembering the dreams sometimes brings on anxiety. But I have learned to control it."

"Wouldn't it be better to just not remember the dreams? That's what's making you all twitchy in the first place."

"But I am trying to find the root of them."

"I still don't understand why you want to go to Oyen."

"It is hard to explain. At times I feel like a sleepwalker living inside a dream. I keep thinking that if I can reach Oyen I might be able to wake up."

Here was one strange little dude. There's always one or two of them hanging around at every truck stop.

"You kinda remind me of this one fellow, also had long red hair, who tried to cadge a ride off Two-Gun Billy once when I was with him. Walked right up to us at a gas station and claimed he needed to get to some commune in the Kootenays so he could become born again. Two-Gun Billy didn't like the looks of him, but was polite all the same. He pointed to me and told the hippie that he already had a passenger. *That's right,* I said. *I'm running away from home, thumbing my way to Vancouver.* I was all of eight years old. That hippie just looked down and said that Jesus loved me and then walked off."

To her surprise Milo slapped his knee, threw his head back and let out a strange kind of hiccup-like laughter.

"What the hell is so funny about that?"

"I get it now," said Milo, trying to catch his breath. "Two-Gun Billy never broke the law, but sometimes he bent it." He nodded profusely. "Yes, that is a good one."

Mavis Jean gave him a queer look. Unzipping her duffel bag, she began to rummage through it.

"What are you looking for?" he asked.

"A little travelling companion." She produced a small zippered leather-bound Bible. "This is my travelling Bible. I used to take it with me when I went on the road with Two-Gun Billy."

"Did he read to you?"

"Two-Gun Billy never had much use for religion. No, I used to play a game with it. Here, I'll show you."

Milo clapped his hands. "I like games."

She unzipped the Bible and held it up in the air. "First I ask a question. *Will I find a ride home today*?" She let the Bible fall open in her hand to a random page, circled her finger in the air and let it fall on the page. "And there's the answer to my question."

Milo leaned closer with a quizzical expression, craning his neck to see the page. "What does it say?"

Mavis Jean read it aloud: "*After Saul returned from pursuing the Philistines, he was told, 'David is in the desert of En Gedi.' So Saul took three thousand chosen men from all and set out to look for David and his men near the Crags of the Wild Goats.*"

Milo thought about this for a moment. "I do not understand."

"Hello? Are you deaf or what?" Mavis Jean zipped up the Bible in disgust. "Saul took three thousand men to look for David. I'd say it's dollars to donuts I'll find that ride."

She stuffed the travelling Bible back into the duffel bag and zipped it closed. With some effort she rose to her feet.

"Where are you going?" asked Milo. "I want to ask the Bible a question."

"Gotta circulate," she said. "Sure as hell ain't gonna find that ride sitting round here jawing with you." She ambled toward the cafeteria's big glass doors. They were streaked with a cruel glare, reflecting a scorched and empty sky.

2

Vesta Bates stood before the door of her brother's bedroom. She was still in her dressing gown, her hair long and loose and not yet twisted into the punishing bun she presented to the world. Bill's doctor commented on how weary she was looking whenever he saw her. He often suggested putting Bill into respite care so she could get a break, but she would have none of it. She'd been taking care of him long before his first stroke, ever since both of their parents had perished in an automobile accident when she was twelve and he was seven.

She gently rapped against the door with a leathery knuckle before opening it a crack and sidling into the dim room. He was already awake, staring up at the ceiling. The skin on his face settled back when he was lying down, straightening out the lopsided mask of partial paralysis.

"Good morning, Bill."

His eyeballs shifted slowly to look at her face and followed as she crossed over to the window.

"Brace yourself now."

She tugged on the pulley cord and the curtains parted, flooding the room with sunlight. Bill's eyelids fluttered and squinted the way moths dance before a restless flame. His good arm jerked up, as if of its own mind, to shade his eyes.

"I warned you, didn't I? You'll get used to it in a minute."

She drew back the old grey-and-red horse blanket, the same one he had kept in the sleeping compartment of his rig all the years he had driven for White Line. Since those days, holes had been patched over countless times and the edges were becoming ever more tattered and frayed. The blanket was also due for another cleaning. Vesta always took care to wash it by hand, fearing the old Kenmore in the basement might shred it beyond repair.

"You want my help or do you want to give it a try yourself first?"

"Me firs'." The words slithered out of a trembling slit formed by the corner of his mouth that was still capable of movement.

He gamely tried to shift himself, balancing on his good arm. The other arm, thinner and sallow from disuse, resembled a rotting branch. The velour robe he always slept in was bunching up above the knees as his thin legs—birch-white with ropy blue veins—edged closer to the side of the bed. By the time his feet were dangling above the floor, one of his socks had twisted itself so that the wool heel puffed out at his ankle.

"Haven't seen you this full of beans in a good long while." She helped him sit up the rest of the way. "Now let's get some clothes on you."

It took almost twenty minutes these days to dress her brother. The first thing she did was retrieve a fresh pair of boxer shorts and socks from his top bureau drawer and knelt before him.

"C'mon now, lift them up."

Bill lifted one foot at a time so she could pull off the socks he had worn to bed and slip on the clean ones. She eased the leg holes of the boxers over each of his feet and hiked the underpants up to his knees. Clutching her narrow shoulder, Bill half-stood so she could tug them the rest of the way up.

"We're making record time this morning, but mind you don't tucker yourself out before the day has even begun."

Opening the closet door, she chose a pair of faded blue jeans and a short-sleeved shirt from the sparse selection of clothes dangling from plastic hangers. The cowboy boots he once declared would have to be pried off his cold dead feet were relegated to a permanent corner of the closet. He wore only the red corduroy slippers that waited by the night table.

Getting him out of his robe and into the jeans and shirt was accomplished with a minimum of fuss. He helped by using his good hand to lift his paralyzed arm for easier access in and out of sleeves. Although it was faster for Vesta to do up the tricky shirt buttons, it was a matter of pride for Bill that his good hand still had the strength and dexterity to zip up and snap his jeans.

He was also still able to wash his own face, comb his hair and brush his teeth in the bathroom down the hall. This gave Vesta enough time to dress herself in a crisp summer skirt and blouse and to put up her hair. She had never figured out the application of make-up or fancy scents. Mascara and lipstick somehow made her look more homely. Even the more expensive fragrances simply turned her stomach. She needed to be ready before Bill finished his ablutions so she could hurry downstairs before him.

Despite his dependence on her, he stubbornly insisted on negotiating the staircase alone. She reasoned that if he was going to tumble to his death it would be better if she was already down there, rather than having to rush down after him and possibly fall herself. She tried to allay her fears by having a thick rubber tread tacked securely along the length of the stairs.

After fetching that morning's *Drumheller Mail* from the slot under their mailbox, she watched Bill's measured descent from the bottom of the staircase. His good hand was pressed flat against the wall and his body was angled in such a way that the dead weight of the paralyzed arm offered a kind of ballast. Vesta held her breath as his foot hovered in mid-air—until he had taken that last step onto the bottom.

Breakfast was a cup of coffee slurped through a corner of his mouth, a bowl of oatmeal and a glass of water to wash down his daily dosage of pills.

He then retreated to the porch and took his usual place in the rattan chair with the wide fanned-out back. He had bought it outside of Vancouver at a shop that imported goods from the Pacific Rim. The seat was solidly woven, but only moderately comfortable, so Vesta had sewn a special foam cushion for him.

At one time she tried to cajole him into doing his speech exercises on the porch, hoping the fresh air would make them less of a chore. But he was too embarrassed to do them out in the open, even though there weren't many people around who would see him. After the second stroke he stopped doing the exercises altogether.

The porch became his last refuge. His only pleasure was to roll and smoke one cigarette after another, which he did one-handed, the way he used to while driving his rig. Sitting on the porch was the only place where Bill could hold onto some semblance of his old self. This morning Vesta stepped out to join him and stood with one hand on the metal railing.

"Sure is one beautiful morning." She surveyed the expanse of lawn that surrounded the house and slanted down towards the road. "Grass sure needs a good cutting."

Theirs was one of the few houses situated on the northern outskirts of Drumheller, a few miles from the on-ramp that led to Highway 9 going east toward Hanna. The only other house in view was the Cochrane farm across the road. Tammy Cochrane was outside hanging laundry on the line. She stopped to wave at them. Vesta waved back. Bill simply raised the index finger of his good hand as if testing the direction of the wind.

"I'll have to remember to take over some brownies and see if young Danny can come by with his power mower."

"Walnuss." He slipped out a rolling paper from the booklet on the small foldout table. There was also an open tin of tobacco, a lighter and an ashtray.

"Now, Bill, you know Danny has a nut allergy. But I'll make an extra batch with walnuts for you."

Bill used the rolling paper to pinch a wad of tobacco from the tin and rolled up a cigarette with surprising dexterity. Vesta looked over and grudgingly admired the cigarette. It was firm and straight with not a single wrinkle in the white paper. When he lit it she looked away, but smelled the calm curl of grey smoke—sweetish and solitary.

"There's something I've been meaning to tell you." She watched Tammy Cochrane taking clothes pegs from her mouth to clip onto a large bed sheet on the line. "Mavis Jean's coming home."

He puffed on his cigarette but made no reply. There was a slight whistling noise, like dry wind through brush, when he exhaled the smoke.

"It'll be good for her to be home again, don't you think?"

He rolled the tip of his cigarette against the rim of the ashtray.

"You can't still be mad about the way she left. I know there's a part of you wanting to see her again."

Tammy Cochrane waved again and carried her empty laundry basket into the house. Although the morning was beginning to swelter without the slightest breath of a breeze, Vesta thought she could see a slight ripple across the bed sheet hanging on the clothesline. Maybe it was just a trick of the sunlight.

"She's been wandering aimlessly for too long. She needs to be in the bosom of her family."

The sun angled its intensity onto the bed sheet in such a way as to make it slightly transparent. Vesta was able to make out the contours of low shrubs that circled part way behind and around the Cochranes' house.

"There are times when I can't help wondering, Bill. Did we do the right thing not telling her? Maybe it would've been better if she knew the truth."

She turned to her brother and saw something harden in his slack expression. He stubbed out his cigarette and immediately began to roll another.

3

In the cafeteria's men's room Milo was hunched over one of the white porcelain sinks, splashing cold water on his face, chest, arms and armpits. He slipped the bandana off his head, soaked it under the running tap and wrung it out. Two truckers stood at urinals, staring at the scummy grout between the tiles in front of them. A man in plaid shorts held a little boy up to the automatic hand dryer. The boy squealed with delight as he shook his wet hands limply under the jet of hot air.

Milo studied himself in the mirror. He was red from the sun, having spent the morning shirtless in the parking lot. His mess of dark orange hair reminded him of a cartoon thermometer with the mercury exploding out of the top.

He could feel heat emanating from his body, reminding him of stories about people spontaneously combusting and imagined himself as a walking time bomb that might go off at any minute. He plugged up the basin's drain hole with his drenched bandana and filled the sink with water, dunking his face in up to his ears and holding it there, the way people on television immerse ticking packages into swimming pools or bathtubs.

"Nothing like cold water on a scorcher like today."

Milo lifted his head and wiped the dripping water from his eyes. The speaker was a stocky, unshaven man at the next sink. He filled his cupped hands with water from the tap and splashed it over his blunt face. Milo hadn't noticed him before. He seemed to materialize from nowhere. His uncombed hair needed a trim and his denim shirttails hung out like a wrinkled loincloth.

"I hope no one minds me doing this here," said Milo. "I know this is a public bathroom."

"A fellow travelling by his thumb needs to clean up as much as anyone else. You know they got showers upstairs?"

"I thought they were only for truckers."

"I don't think nobody'd mind if you used them."

The man filled his hands again, swished the water violently in his mouth and spit it out in a hard jet that rang against the drain's metal rim. "Where you headed?"

"Oyen."

"I once had a girlfriend from Oyen. Said she learned the facts of life from watching the bulls and heifers on her father's ranch."

Raspy laughter swelled from his gaping bullhorn of a mouth. Milo could smell fumes of liquor coming from the man's breath. The man spit into the sink and asked: "How long you been travelling?"

"Almost two weeks."

"Long time to be on the road. Don't you worry, I'll fix you up with a ride."

"Are you going to Oyen?" Milo asked hopefully.

"No." The man nudged the automatic dryer's huge shiny button with his elbow. He had to raise his voice to be heard over the hot air rushing out of the chrome nozzle. "But I know all the truckers who come through here."

Once his hands were dry he stuck one of them out towards Milo. The hand was brown and burnt by the sun and still damp. "The name's Ned."

"I am Milo."

Ned tightened his grasp for a second longer than was comfortable. "Don't worry, sport, I'll get you outta here. Meet me near the parking lot entrance at midnight. By the cement pylons. You know where I mean?"

"Yes," said Milo. "I think so."

Ned winked at him. "Old Ned won't let you down. I'm expecting you now."

Before Milo could say anything else Ned was out the door.

Milo unplugged his bandana from the sink and the water spiralled down the drain. He wrung the bandana out well and fastened it around his head pirate-style. Taking up his backpack, he went into one of the stalls and locked the door behind him.

The backpack was propped against the door, giving him a better sense of security. He took his notebook from one of the pack's outer pouches and opened to the page he had been writing on this morning. His handwriting was meticulous but tiny—to the point of being almost illegible to anyone else. He could fill an ordinary page with double of what someone with regular-sized writing could fit.

> *I believe last night's dream to be a breakthrough of sorts. I have not dreamt of the cattle carcasses since leaving St. Tom's. At one point Dr. Veldt believed that they might signify a wish to shed the past, a longing for some kind of rebirth. I think this could be significant. A need for orderliness, for purpose. Dr. Veldt says that one cannot ignore external stimuli when trying to analyze a dream. So I think it is important to note that I had been asleep in a sitting position. It was a very uncomfortable night and I woke up stiff and aching. Still, the overall feeling from this dream was a strange sense of hopefulness. Because I dreamt of the cattle again. I was afraid I had lost them. Afraid I had lost my purpose. So many times I had thought about turning around and going back to Toronto. Back to St. Tom's and Dr. Veldt. But now my faith is renewed. I wasn't wrong to leave everything behind.*

Milo closed the notebook, took a deep breath and began to feel calmer. It was so peaceful sitting in the stall. Back at St. Tom's the only real privacy he could ever find was in the bathroom. The problem of overcrowding was chronic, resulting in an ebb and flow of the same patients being prematurely discharged only to be admitted once again a few months later when life on the outside proved to be too difficult. At St. Tom's Milo often found himself moving slowly. Each motion measured under the fluorescent ceiling's clinical sheen. The washed-out plaster walls, the seamless tile floors, the nurses' station made of glass and chrome. He was constantly aware that there was no sense of traction, no way to grip on to any surface. From the moment he entered St.

Tom's he felt as if he had been sucked into its inner world as smoothly as the slot of a candy machine ingests a coin.

His reverie was broken by the sharp metal clank of the stall door next to him. The rusty scrape and click of the bolt being slid into place. The heavy jangling of a belt being unbuckled followed by the sharp whiz of a fly being unzipped. A guttural sigh.

Milo peered down at the space under the partition between his stall and the next. He could make out a heavy black boot, buffed to a spit-and-polish sheen, with a thick leather sole and blunt toe. On top of it rested a blue-black trouser cuff. A good sturdy material sporting the single yellow stripe of some kind of uniform.

Despite the fluttering panic—a trapped bird lodged between his breastbone and rib cage—Milo managed to extricate himself and the bulky backpack from the narrow stall and slipped out of the bathroom.

He crammed the notebook into his back pocket.

In the corridor he had a clear view of the glass front doors and was able to spot the patrol car in the smaller parking lot. At a nearby table he saw a police officer casually sipping a cup of coffee. Milo had no doubt that the person in the bathroom stall was his partner.

Startled by a bang from inside the bathroom, Milo realized the partner would soon be coming out. He thrust his arms through the straps of the backpack without bothering to get them all the way up onto his shoulders. He hurried along the corridor and slipped out through the back door.

4

Curtis took two frosty cans of Molson from the cooler between the driver and passenger seats in his cab and handed one to Mavis Jean. She immediately rolled the icy aluminium against her forehead.

"You don't want to let that get too warm." Curtis pulled the tab on his can, producing a whispered *yesss*. He took a long swig, groaned and belched deep from the back of his throat. Flecks of foam clung to the coarse fringe of his drooping moustache. A couple of drops slid down his chin and darkened the tank top. There was still a hardness in the curve of his slight pot-belly.

"Don't get any better'n that." He wiped his chin with the back of his hand.

Mavis Jean took a healthy swallow of beer and followed with her own slow, wet belch. "Like rainwater cutting through a dust-caked gutter."

Curtis took a pack of Players from the dashboard, slid it open and held it out to Mavis Jean. There were only four left and she hesitated.

"Go on. I got a whole unopened carton back there." He jerked a thumb at the cab's sleeping compartment where Mavis Jean had stowed her duffel bag.

They helped themselves to cigarettes. Mavis Jean whipped out her lighter.

"So, you still looking for a ride to Drumheller?" he asked.

"Sure am."

"You ever been up that giant dinosaur they got?"

She snorted out a small cloud of smoke. "Nah."

"I was reading about that thing. It's 86 feet high and they used 65,000 pounds of steel to make it. There's about 106 steps to climb to get to the top. Supposed to be the best view of the badlands."

"Best view of the badlands is through the windshield of a Peterbilt," corrected Mavis Jean.

"I roger that. Still, I'd climb up that dinosaur just to say I'd done it."

"Good for tourism and the economy and all that, I guess. But I never went in much for that stuff myself."

"Dinosaurs?" asked Curtis, moving closer to her.

"Tourists," she answered, meeting him halfway. They kissed.

Curtis popped two more cans and handed one to Mavis Jean. "I'm due to pick up a load in Calgary in a couple of days." He blew two perfectly round smoke rings against the windshield where they instantly began to dissolve on impact, leaving a barely visible haze. "I can pretty much drop you off at your front door."

His grey eyes were cold and clear like a wolf's but with a brown smokiness around the edges, something warm and smouldering against the ice.

"I'm leaving first thing in the morning," he said.

"Sooner the better." She clinked her beer can against his and drained it.

Curtis wasn't a company driver. He owned his rig, or most of it anyway. He still had to pay off the bank for another year. Mavis Jean had admired the fancy red lettering on the white driver's door that read: KING OF THE ROAD. It had been adorned with a hand-painted sky-blue vista complete with majestic clouds and a blazing golden sun. Beneath the lettering was a curving stretch of blacktop with a white line down the middle disappearing into infinity. Curtis freelanced as a custom auto painter when there were no trucking jobs. "But ain't nothing I like more than barrelling down a stretch of blacktop."

The coppery blend of tobacco and beer on his warm breath wafted lazily into Mavis Jean's consciousness. She breathed deeply and felt the tight corners of her mouth naturally stretch upwards

"I hear you," she said. "You're running with the big dogs and no mistake."

"You like to be on the move."

"If you don't keep moving you get stuck. Ain't nothing left then but to shrivel up and die."

"That what's happened to your daddy?"

"May as well have." The words seemed to be swallowed up by the blistering day.

"Sorry." said Curtis. "I didn't mean to—"

"Forget it." She waved her hand dismissively.

"How long's it been since you last saw him?"

"Almost five years now. Spring of '02."

She took a drag on her cigarette. The white paper burned dangerously close to the filter line. "Last time I saw him he was pushing his spoon round in a bowl of cooling porridge. My Aunt Vesta had to run some errands in the station wagon that morning, so it was left to me to watch him."

She rolled down the window and tossed out the smouldering filter. She reached for the pack of Players and lit up another.

"I pleaded with him to eat, but he kept staring down at his porridge like it was a pit of quicksand and he was sinking up to his neck. Finally I reached across the table and was about to take the bowl away when he lifted his spoon high in the air and smashed it down into the porridge. It was splattered across the table and onto the front of his shirt."

Curtis popped open two more beers.

"I wiped up the front of his shirt and cleaned the table. Then I took his shirt off and went up to his room to fetch a clean one. He had this puzzled look on his face like he had no idea what was going on."

"That's a damn shame." Curtis put his hand on hers. She let it stay there.

"When I was upstairs looking for a clean shirt in his closet I found his old duffel bag rolled up in the corner of the shelf. Same one he used to take on the road. He used to let me pack his clothes into it whenever he went away and unpack it when he came back home. There was always a present waiting for me somewhere in that jumble of clothes.

"It was so weird to see the old duffel bag rolled up, kinda like it was hibernating. I remember unrolling it and thinking it was like the thick hide of an animal that had been skinned and cleaned. Waiting to have life breathed into it again."

Curtis gently squeezed her wrist and tried to manoeuvre her closer to him. She pulled back and he took a swig of beer.

"Next thing I knew I was in my room grabbing everything in my drawers and closet and stuffing them into the bag. None of the careful folding and packing like I used to do for him. I jammed everything down that duffel bag's craw like it was a big old snake and wrestled it to the floor to zip the thing up. I didn't even think of my daddy sitting in the kitchen in his undershirt. I was out the door and heading for the highway."

"You just left him there?"

"I ain't proud of it." She sucked on her cigarette and drew hot smoke down her throat. She could feel it scalding her lungs and searing into her heart.

"Well, don't you worry." Curtis rested his hand against her knee. "I'll get you home soon enough."

After pounding back the rest of her beer, she opened the passenger door and stepped down onto the pavement.

"Hey! Did I say something wrong?"

"My stuff safe with you?"

"Sure it is. Where you going?"

"I won't be long." She used the heel of her hand to slam the passenger door shut before Curtis could ask any more questions.

5

Mavis Jean found herself running across the parking lot and slowed down once she reached the semicircle of lawn in front of the truck stop complex. She took a moment to notice the white elm where she had sat with that red-haired kid with the do-rag. He wasn't there now and the tree looked strangely bare without him.

She pushed open the glass doors.

Inside, the drop in temperature was a welcome shock to her system. She could hear the roaring air-conditioner motor and thought of a jet idling on a tarmac. Icy needles of sweat began to prickle the back of her neck. She sneezed.

A police officer sitting in a nearby booth in the cafeteria looked up at her. "Bless you." He was dark with broad Indian cheekbones and eyes blue as a calm lake.

"Thanks," she said. "It's like a meat locker in here."

"You just need a minute to get used to it. All the same you have to be careful of those sudden changes in temperature. That's how you get sick."

"Too true."

She continued on into the corridor, stopping at one of the pay phones by the bathrooms. The door to the men's room swung open and out stepped another police officer, most likely the partner of the one she had just spoken to. This one was a burly fellow with a reddish toothbrush moustache and beady dark eyes. He strode past Mavis Jean without looking at her. She had heard all about the whole good cop/bad cop routine and had no difficulty imagining which role he suited best.

She picked up the pay phone's receiver and held it to her ear. The dial tone's flat hum matched the drone of anxiety inside her. The tip of her index finger pressed zero and then dialled the home number. A recorded voice asked her to say her name. She did. It rang once and Vesta accepted the charges.

"Hello?" she said.

"Hi, it's me," answered Mavis Jean. She glimpsed a crack of light at the end of the dark corridor. The back door was ajar.

"Where are you?" asked Vesta.

"Dauphin." There was something on the floor, illuminated by the crack of daylight. "Looks like I've got a ride home."

"Really? Your daddy will be so glad to hear that."

She squinted and made out the thing on the floor to be a notebook. "How's Two-Gun Billy doing?"

"He's having one of his better days today."

"That's good."

"So how long 'til you get home?"

"I'm not sure." Mavis Jean couldn't take her eyes off the notebook. Someone must have dropped it. "We're leaving first thing in the morning."

"Who you riding with?"

"Just a trucker. His name is Curtis."

"I don't have to worry, do I?"

"Aunt Vesta."

"I'm sorry, dear. I know you can take care of yourself. After all, you take after your daddy."

"Has he said anything? About me coming home and all?"

"He misses you. He can't wait to see you again. We both can't wait."

"Me too." Mavis Jean realized she had stretched the metal phone cord all the way, moving toward the notebook. "I better go now. I'll try to call again."

After she hung, up she went to the back door and looked out onto the alley. There was no one around. The door faced a large blue Dumpster. She picked up the notebook. The writing inside was tiny and she had to squint to make out the words. What she did manage to decipher described a dream about dead cattle. A rustling noise came from inside the Dumpster.

She stepped out into the alley and read aloud from the notebook, "*Last night I dreamed of the cattle again.*"

There was more movement and then a head peered over the edge of the Dumpster. It was the red-haired kid. "That is mine," he said.

"This?" She held up the notebook.

"Can I have it back please?" He reached a hand down towards her.

"Ain't you coming down outta there?"

He looked around the alley. "Is it safe?"

"Safe? You hiding from someone?"

"Are they still around?"

"Who?"

"I saw a police car out front," he said, lowering his head. "There are policemen in the cafeteria."

She tilted back her cowboy hat with the notebook. "You running from the law?"

"Please, can I have my notebook? Please?" He waved his hand impatiently and there was an edge of panic in his voice.

She thrust the notebook at him. "No need to get your panties in a knot."

He reached for it and she pulled it back.

"That is not fair," he cried.

"If you want it so bad maybe you should come down and get it yourself." She waved it just out of his reach. "Ain'tcha worried you'll catch some kind of disease in there?"

"Is it safe?"

"Ain't nobody out here but me." She stretched out her arms to prove her point.

"Those policemen might still be around."

"The only APB those boys are checking out is on a refill on a cuppa joe."

"But my name is Milo."

She shook her head in bewilderment. "Then I guess that puts you in the clear."

"Could you help me down?"

"You climbed up there your own self, you'll have to climb out the same way."

"At least help me with my backpack."

With some difficulty he hoisted the bulky thing over his head and eased it over the side of the Dumpster.

"Can I let go?" he asked.

"Bombs away, Snoopy."

As he released the backpack, Mavis Jean stepped aside. The backpack thudded against the ground and bounced once.

"Hey, you promised—"

"Just get your skinny butt down here before you get hauled away to the city dump."

Milo balanced on the rim of the Dumpster—all at once losing his footing—and landed on top of his backpack, spilling ass over teakettle. There was a small gash below his knee.

"How'd you do that?" Mavis Jean asked.

"On the corner of the Dumpster when I was climbing in. It is just a scratch."

"Maybe you should put something on it."

Milo sat on his backpack and inspected the wound. Mavis Jean couldn't help but wince. "What made you think those cops were after you?"

"I thought Dr. Veldt might have sent them."

"I think you mentioned him before."

"I was under his care at St. Tom's."

She narrowed her eyes. "That a hospital?"

"St. Thomas' Mental Health Centre in Toronto. I was there six months."

"What for?"

"I was diagnosed as having an acute form of general anxiety disorder."

"What's that mean?"

"I was afraid," he explained.

"Of what?"

"I don't know. Everything and nothing. At first he prescribed Valium and later on Ativan. They made me constipated and I couldn't sleep."

"I think Two-Gun Billy takes Valium. He takes all kinds of different pills."

Milo was tentatively touching the gash on his leg and flinching.

"You really ought to clean that out," said Mavis Jean.

He covered the gash with one hand and laid his other hand on top, then interlaced the fingers of both hands.

"It was in St. Tom's that I started dreaming about the slaughtered cattle. I thought it was a side effect from the medication. But Dr. Veldt found the dreams very interesting. Then I discovered the newspaper article I showed you."

"So this headshrinker told you to go to Oyen?"

"No." He was putting pressure on the wound with both his hands. He gritted his teeth. "I got out of St. Tom's on my own."

"You mean escaped?"

"I walked out, really."

"Walked out?" She snapped her fingers. "Like that?"

"Yes." Milo gasped and bit his lip. He put pressure on the gash, his interlaced fingers tensing up, the knuckles rigidly white. "But Dr Veldt thinks I should still be there."

"Why?"

As Mavis Jean looked on in horrified fascination, Milo closed his eyes and gripped his leg as if he was trying to set a broken bone. Then, as quickly as he'd begun, he stopped.

"Come on," she said. "You need to get that gash cleaned up."

When he unlaced his fingers the only evidence that there had ever been a wound was the purplish crescent-moon of a scar.

6

Two-Gun Billy lay in bed gazing at bits of sky between the leaves of the cottonwood tree outside his window. It was a deep shade of sky—what might be the final greyish-blue of evening or just as easily the first bluish-grey of morning.

The water in the bathroom stopped running and Lynette stepped out wearing the white satin robe with the lace trim he'd bought her. He was mesmerized by her brilliant hair: the colour of blood oranges. Some women tied up their hair at night or stuffed it into tight nets or caps, but Lynette wouldn't think of it. Two-Gun Billy saw it as an outright blessing to be able to sleep beside such beautiful flowing red hair, imagining he was sleeping beside a rushing river of fire.

"Feel." She pressed his palm against the slight but perfect roundness of her belly. The satin was thin and he could feel her warmth through it. Then something moved. And again. Something struggling to get out. Something strong and alive.

"Feel that?" she said. "That's your son."

He looked up at her, puzzled. "How you know that?"

"I guess a woman sometimes naturally knows these things."

Two-Gun Billy raised one disbelieving eyebrow, unable to suppress a smile that broadened across his narrow spade of a face. He knew how she loved to tease him. Once more he placed his sinewy hand against her belly and felt a sudden kick coming from within.

"You don't know if that's a boy or a girl," he said.

"What's the matter, don't you want a son?"

"'Course I do." He tried to touch her again but she had moved beyond his reach. Wanting to sit up, he shifted onto his left arm and found that it wouldn't support him. "Damn! I must've done something wicked awful to this hand."

Lynette sat at her vanity table, applying moisturizing cream to her face. Her reflection in the make-up mirror gave him a withering glance. "Seems like your body's got a longer memory than your brain."

"My brain's just as fit as any part of my body."

"But you don't remember how you hurt your hand, do you?"

"Sure I do." He scratched his head. "Just gimme a minute."

"Honestly." She worked a generous amount of cream into the pores of her high forehead while trying to massage away the wrinkles she imagined to be there. "You men only think with your fists or with what's between your legs. You punched Earl Porter Lawrence the other day."

He focused on a corner of the ceiling, hoping it might help him to remember. "Slick dude from Toronto. Fancy stickpin and matching cuff links."

"He's also an important promoter who's interested in booking us at the Canadian National Exhibition." She wiped the cream from her face and began to apply talcum powder to her shoulders and under her arms. "Or at least he was interested until you blackened the poor man's eye."

"I did it defending your honour."

"All he did was pay me a compliment. It was all very innocent."

"The way he was giving you the glad eye didn't look all that innocent."

Lynette rolled her eyes and shook her head. "Sometimes a little bit of flirting is the price of doing business." She turned to him. "He wanted to give us work. In *Toronto*? It could've been a big break."

"We do alright out here."

In one swift movement Lynette scooped up the jar of moisturizer from the vanity table and hurled it at Two-Gun Billy. It smashed against the wall just above the headboard, leaving a creamy white glob.

"*You* do all right, but me and your unborn child—*your son!*—deserve better."

Two-Gun Billy scrambled to sit up, but his useless hand would do nothing to support him. "You don't know for sure that that's a boy you're carrying!"

"Have you been listening to anything I've said?"

Lynette was standing now. She hurled a hairbrush that whizzed past Two-Gun Billy's ear and bounced off a corner of the headboard. He felt like he was in the middle of one of those bad dreams where no matter how hard you try your body is barely able to move and every part of you feels weighed down like sacks of wet sand.

She kicked over the chair she'd been sitting in. "Thanks to you and your stupid jealousy, all my dreams of a better life are finished for good."

"I'll give you everything. You'll never be wanting for anything with me."

She stood still and he dared to hope the storm had blown over.

"How are you ever going to be able to do anything with that bum hand of yours? How do you know you're ever going to be able to shoot again?"

"Of course I'll be able to shoot again," he protested. "It'll be right as rain in a few days."

"Earl Porter Lawrence takes the train back to Toronto the day after tomorrow." Her voice had a tone of decisiveness he found unnerving.

"Let him take the train straight to hell for all I care."

"Before he leaves, one of us is going to apologize to him."

"It sure as hell ain't gonna be me."

"Suit yourself then."

She took a pair of stockings from her dresser drawer, one of her good dresses from the closet and went into the bathroom, locking the door behind her.

"What are you doing? Lynette?"

He waited but there was no answer from the behind the bathroom door. That was the worst thing of all. To hear nothing but silence.

"Lynette? You can't get dressed now."

He could hear his own voice hanging in the air.

"Lynette, come to bed," he cried. "You hear me?"

He listened intently to what she was doing in the bathroom.

"Answer me, Lynette!"

He grew frightened as if he was shouting down a deep and dark chasm she had fallen into and wondering whether he should jump in after her.

"Lynette! Lynette! Lynette!"

A door opened. A tall, ramrod-straight silhouette stood against the light.

"Bill?"

This was not Lynette's voice.

"Bill? Is everything alright? Do you need another blanket?"

Vesta came into the room and helped him lay his head back down on the pillow. She pulled his old grey-and-red horse blanket up to his chin.

"Try to go to sleep now, Bill. You were just having a bad dream."

The door closed.

His left hand, the paralyzed one, lay under the blanket, tucked in for the night. He held up his good right hand, its silhouette stark against the light of the full moon filling up a corner of the window. He reached out, as if touching the glowing satiny white curve, imagining he could feel a warmth against his palm. And something moving. Something strong. Alive.

7

Curtis was curled up and snoring in third gear as Mavis Jean slipped out of bed. The green glowing dial of a travel alarm clock showed 12:15. She watched her reflection in the dark window as she dressed. Almost an out-of-body experience.

Here she was in another strange room with another strange body in the bed. The familiarity chilled her blood. Despite the summer heat she sensed a crystalline quality to everything. Even in the parking lot below, the chrome grilles seemed to give off a frozen silver haze like breath in winter.

She was able to see well enough to find her way around the room. Curtis' jeans were draped over the back of a chair. She felt around until she located one of the front pockets and took out a ring of keys. Misjudging the weight, she nearly dropped it and the sudden jangling —a frenzied flapping of tiny metallic wings—was enough to stop her heart. She squeezed the entire ring in her fist and stood motionless, jagged teeth biting into the fleshy part of her palm as a warning to be more careful.

Curtis grunted, rolling over with bedsprings groaning beneath him, and pulled the blanket around his shoulders. He mumbled something (to Mavis Jean it sounded like *Haven't got it on me now.*) and let out a long, high-pitched fart before finally settling down again.

In her head she rehearsed what she'd say in case he did wake up. She wanted to get her travelling Bible from her duffel bag in the sleeping compartment of his rig. Truth was, after he'd pushed himself between her legs and immediately rolled over into a coma, she had lain awake for two hours, thinking about going back home after all these years. Thinking about seeing Two-Gun Billy again, probably for the last time. She was feeling more alone than she'd ever been. She liked having the travelling Bible close at hand. Playing her question-and-answer game took the edge off her loneliness.

She picked up her boots and inched the door open, squinting at the hallway's washed-out fluorescent glare. She edged through the door's slim gap so as not to let any of the harsh light enter the room.

Outside, the mugginess was an invisible cobweb hanging in the air. She made her way to Curtis' rig. As she was going through all the keys on the ring to find the one that opened the passenger door, she heard voices in the distance. They seemed to be coming from the parking lot entrance.

The perimeter of the parking lot was lined with flickering lampposts, most of which were partially obscured by clouds of mosquitoes. Near one of them she could see two figures. One was stocky, powerful looking. The other looked thinner and was wearing a bulky pack. He was closer to the light and Mavis Jean recognized Milo. She couldn't make out what they were saying, but Milo kept shaking his head. When he tried to walk away, the stocky one grabbed his arm and raised his voice. She thought she heard him say something about the two of them having a deal.

Mavis Jean knew the best thing would be for her to retrieve her Bible from the sleeper and leave. Even so, she stuffed the ring of keys into a front pocket and found herself walking toward them.

"Milo?" she called out. "Everything okay?"

The stocky one took a cigarette from behind his ear and dug a lighter from a back pocket. The momentary flame illuminated the shadowy blueness of his unshaven jaw and the hard ridge of his thick eyebrows. Something about his lopsided grin made the back of Mavis Jean's neck go cold and prickly. He took a moment to give her the once-over.

"Who the hell are you?" The liquor on his breath seemed to warp the air in a single toxic wave.

"Mavis Jean?" said Milo. "What are you doing here?"

"Never mind that," she said. "Who's this?"

"This is Ned," Milo explained. "He offered to find me a lift."

"How do you know him?" she asked.

"We're old buddies from way back," said Ned.

"I met him this afternoon," said Milo. "He has a friend who will drive me to Oyen. But now he is asking me for money."

"Is he now?" Mavis Jean folded her arms and fixed Ned with a cold stare.

"Call it a finder's fee," said Ned.

"A scam is more like it." Mavis Jean took Milo by the hand. "C'mon, we're getting outta here."

Ned stepped towards them. "Whoa there. Me and sport here had a deal."

"One more step, I'll boot you so hard you'll have three Adam's apples."

The sound of a motor growled nearby, followed by a set of headlights slicing through the darkness. A quarter-ton pickup rolled into the parking lot. Ned stuck two fingers in his mouth and let out a piercing whistle.

"Who's that?" said Mavis Jean.

"That's your ride, sport. Hope I don't have to tell him he came all the way here for nothing."

"Tell him whatever you want," said Mavis Jean and took Milo by wrist. But just as they turned to go, the truck pulled up and stopped directly in their path.

Milo stumbled backward, the weight of his backpack pulling him off balance. His wrist jerked loose from Mavis Jean's grip and he crashed down onto the pavement, landing on the backpack, arms and legs flailing as he rocked helplessly like a flipped-over turtle.

Ned threw his head back and howled with laughter, drumming on both thighs with his open palms and doubling over until he was gasping for breath.

Mavis Jean grabbed both of Milo's arms and yanked him up with such force she feared they would pop out of their sockets.

Pulling away from her, Milo backed off against the wire fence that separated the parking lot from an open field.

"I'm sorry I pulled you up so hard," she said.

He lowered himself into a crouching position and began touching each of his fingertips to his lips.

"What the hell is he doing?" This came from the driver of the pickup, whose elbow protruded out of the window as he propped his doughy head onto the question mark of a fist. He was staring at Milo through greasy strands of hair as limp and colourless as overcooked spaghetti noodles.

"Hey!" said Ned. He moved toward Milo. "What's the deal, sport?"

Mavis Jean stood in Ned's way. "Back off."

Ned held up his hands in mock surrender "I guess she means business."

"Whatever," said the driver. He produced a mickey of whiskey and took a swallow. "Might as well have a little refreshment in the meanwhile."

"Think I'll join you, Glen." Ned parked himself against the pickup's hood and took a swig from the mickey. "Hope you brought some smokes with you."

"Here." Glen tossed a pack to Ned. "Shouldn't you offer the lady a snort?"

Ned held out the bottle to Mavis Jean. "Let's see if we can't all be sociable."

Glen began to whittle a piece of wood with a large hunting knife. It was obvious this little show was for Mavis Jean's benefit. She didn't expect Milo to be of any help and the odds of two against one were enough to convince her to accept the mickey from Ned. She tipped it between pursed lips. The whiskey burned her tongue and throat, settling into a golden simmer deep in her belly.

"What's wrong with that kid?" asked Glen. His blade sliced off a thick spiral of wood as easily as a butter curl.

"Don't worry about him."

"What's that weird shit he's doing with his fingers?"

"Probably just a nervous habit." She tried to hand the mickey back to Ned, but he waved it away and motioned her to take another.

"No problem," he said. "We got all night."

Mavis Jean knew she had to do something soon. She casually brushed her hand against her front pocket, feeling the bulge made by the ring of keys. They weren't much to speak of, but she could do a fair bit of damage. One last pull and she extended the whiskey back to Ned.

He held his hands in the air. "You know what they say, three's a charm. Besides, there's more where that came from. Right, Glen?"

"Got a forty-ouncer in the back."

"Well you'll have to drink it without me."

She tossed the mickey over to Ned. He caught it, but not before some whiskey spilled down his shirt. He rubbed the wet stain with the palm of his hand, smelling and tasting it. Mavis Jean wasn't expecting the laughter that followed—a wheezy staccato, reminding her of drops of water hissing on hot coals.

"You're done drinking when I say." He began walking toward her.

"I don't want any trouble." Her hand felt for the ring of keys.

"Then you better drink up." Ned pressed the mickey against her bottom lip.

"Go on, man!" called Glen. "That babe needs a bottle feeding."

"Okay, okay, okay, you win," said Mavis Jean, smiling.

She drew her hand out of her pocket and jabbed a fistful of keys near Ned's ear, dragging them like metal talons across his jaw. He cried out and tried to shield his face, but before he had a chance, Mavis Jean launched the toe of her boot between his legs. A sharp groan escaped him. He crumpled over and curled up as naturally as a leaf in winter. The mickey smashed against the ground. Mavis Jean could smell the pool of whiskey spreading out on the pavement.

"I guess nobody's gonna be drinking tonight."

"Bitch!"

The door of the pickup flew open and Glen leapt out with the hunting knife held high. Despite his considerable girth, he bounded effortlessly toward her. Before she knew it cold metal seared the side of her neck.

She fell backward, clutching the wound and felt something warm gushing through her fingers. She held her hand up and saw that it was covered in blood.

Ned got to his feet. "Shit, Glen, I think you might've sliced her jugular."

"Screw it," said Glen. "We're outta here."

Mavis Jean couldn't move her head. She heard the sound of footsteps and doors slamming, the roar of an engine and squealing tires. Headlight beams swung above her, blotting out the nighttime sky. She was afraid they were going to run over her. All became dark again as the motor disappeared in the distance.

"Move your hand." Milo knelt beside her and pulled her hand away, then clutched both of his around her neck.

Mavis Jean thought he was trying to choke her. Too weak to struggle, she surrendered to the tightening of his hands around her neck. The stars were pinholes of light shining through the chinks of a black ceiling, hinting at the brilliance of the next world that was awaiting her on the other side. Strangely, she felt secured as if in a brace. His hands formed a kind of tourniquet.

"Try to breathe normally."

She wanted to speak, but the only sound was an intermittent gurgling.

His hands pushed tighter. "This might hurt a bit."

Sweat beaded her hairline and slid down her temples, filling the whorls of her ears. She concentrated on breathing through her nose to lessen the panic building up inside.

"Do not struggle. You will only make it more difficult."

The fever crackled inside her: a severe case of pins and needles spreading from the soles of her feet to the crown of her head. Milo was now straddling her chest. All she could think of was those soft white hands from when they first met that morning, hands that didn't seem to be fit for anything useful. Now she was at their mercy.

Milo's eyes were closed. His breathing was so rapid that the sound solidified into something both senseless and intimate.

Then everything went black.

When her eyes opened again, the stars seemed less intense, almost runny like raindrops on a darkened window. Her neck was sore. When she tried to sit up something sharp twisted through her guts.

"Milo?" Her voice was static and sandpaper.

He was lying beside her in a foetal position, either unconscious or dead. She found his wrist and managed to locate a fluttering pulse.

She lay there holding onto his wrist as if it were a lifeline, as if the two of them were part of some larger constellation linked by the stars.

8

Sunday was Two-Gun Billy's bath night. Although there was a toilet and sink on the upstairs landing, the dull white tub resting on chipped porcelain lion's paws was situated downstairs in a tiny bathroom next to the kitchen.

After his first stroke he continued to enjoy this ablution in private, until the evening he slipped while getting into the tub. Vesta believed, although the doctor couldn't confirm it, that the accident helped to bring on his second stroke. She had a safety bar installed so that he had something to hold onto and remained on hand to offer assistance. As an extra precaution she insisted that he already be in the tub while it was still dry. He would sit there, so scrawny in his nakedness that he could easily slip down the drain if it wasn't plugged, as the water rose around him.

This evening he cupped his good hand under the rushing water.

"Too col'."

Vesta felt the water. "Doesn't feel cold to me, but we can warm it up a bit." She gave the hot water tap an extra turn. "Better?"

He shook his head and stretched to turn the tap even more.

"Come on, Bill, hot water's expensive."

"G'way!" He held onto the tap to prevent her from turning it off.

"That's enough!"

She grabbed his wrist and tried to pry his fingers open. The two of them may as well have been locked in a death struggle for a precious gem or a last morsel of food.

"Stop being so damn stubborn."

He twisted his torso to gain some purchase, but the awkward position proved too strenuous and he had to let go. Vesta turned off the tap.

"You can't say it's cold now."

His silence emanated hurt pride because he was unable to hold his ground.

"I could throw in some carrots and an onion and make a nice soup."

He stared hard at his toes sticking out of the water.

"Here." Vesta soaped up the sponge and handed it to him. "Let me know when you want me to do your back."

She perched herself on the edge of the toilet and turned away to give him a semblance of privacy. The cracks in the corner of the wall by the door reminded her of tiny highways on a map.

"Did I mention that Mavis Jean called today?"

Vesta listened to the odd splash and drip of water as he washed himself.

"Has a ride from Dauphin. Probably be here in a matter of days."

She fingered the corner of a bath towel as if testing the quality of some fine material, silk or possibly satin.

"I remember that first time she phoned after she left. I could tell she was scared. Now that I think about it after all this time, I guess it was pretty brave of her to call in the first place."

Vesta laid the bath towel across her knees. She ran the tips of her fingers across the extra puffy terry cloth, luxuriating in its softness and smoothing out imaginary wrinkles. She was still vaguely aware of the sound of water coming from the tub, playful somehow, like a duck in a pond.

"I'm sure she expected me to lace into her. And I had a good mind to. But I knew if I lost my temper she would never call again. I knew I'd lose her forever."

She began to fold the towel in such a way that the corners met and folded it again until it resembled a small bundle.

"Suddenly I had the urge to tell her right there and then, Bill. The words kept rising up in my throat, like a reaction from all these years of silence."

She rocked the bundle in her arms and tucked in any stray corner that was sticking out or threatening to unravel. Even so, she had the sense that her heart was throbbing against something plush and elaborate, but ultimately empty.

"Sometimes, Bill, I think that maybe deep down she knows."

She heard a soothing trickle, like one of those small indoor fountains. She wondered if Bill had turned on the faucet again and shifted around in time to see the water changing to a lemony yellow

"For the love of ... Bill, why didn't you tell me you had to go?"

The bath water quickly became a deeper kind of orange and then darkened even more. With rising horror it dawned on Vesta that this was blood. Her grip on the bundled towel loosened. It fell open and dropped to the floor.

Bill's moans swelled into shapeless sobs. He ran his fingers through his hair, tugging at the wet strands, while his paralyzed hand hung limply in the tainted bath water. Seeing that broke Vesta's heart as much as it made her want to slap him. She dug her fingers under his armpits and tried to lift him.

"Come on, Bill, grab the safety bar and pull yourself up. I'll help you."

"I ... kaaaah ..."

"Why the hell can't you, Bill?"

"My lez!"

"What about them?"

His words were lost in the infantile wailing that reverberated off the greying tiles. He grabbed on to the safety bar, but Vesta could tell that it was not so much to lift himself up as it was to keep him from sliding further down. There was something wrong with his legs. It was all too much for Vesta to take in. He seemed to be falling apart before her eyes. The water was a murky shade of red, conjuring the image of a Biblical plague.

"Stop crying, Bill," she snapped. "Can't you move your legs at all?"

He shook his head.

The first thing she did was to spread out the bath towel onto the linoleum floor. Then she hoisted her skirt and got down on her knees. There was no way to do this cleanly or easily. She plunged both arms into the mixture of water, piss and blood, hooked one under his legs and used the other to support his back. She tried to hold her breath as the heat from the fetid water rose into her face.

He clung to the safety bar while she managed to lift him partway up.

"Let go, for the love of Pete. I'm trying to get you out."

She balanced him on the edge of the tub while she caught her breath and lowered him onto the bath towel with a hard bump. He cried out.

"Well, what did you expect when I have to do all the work? Now wait here."

He lay there—a gaunt, oversized baby—straining to hold his head up. Vesta went to fetch another towel. When she came back he tried to grab it. "This will go faster if you let me do it."

"I col'."

"I know you're cold. Look at me." She pulled at the sopping front of her blouse. "The sooner I dry you off, the sooner I can dress you."

Fresh underpants, T-shirt and socks lay folded on top of the toilet tank. She wriggled the leg holes of the underpants over his feet and yanked them, bit by bit, up his now motionless legs and under his bony buttocks. She could have been dressing a mannequin or a corpse.

"Naw so ruff."

"Can't help being rough when I'm not getting any help from you."

She went upstairs to fetch a clean sheet, a pillow and the horse blanket from his bed. After she made up the sofa she returned to the bathroom.

"There's no way I'm going to be able to get you upstairs to your room. So it looks like you're going to have to camp out on the sofa for the time being."

She took a deep breath and hooked her hands under his armpits.

"I'm sorry, Bill, but there's only one way to do this."

The bathroom was small, but somehow she manoeuvred him around, dragging him to the living room the way she would a giant rag doll. By the time she lifted him onto the sofa, his socks had slipped halfway off his feet.

Vesta knelt on the floor, sure that every ounce of strength had been drained from her. Two-Gun Billy's paralyzed arm dangled off the side of the sofa. She took the useless hand and caressed her face with the stiff curved fingers.

"Things will be better when Mavis Jean gets here, don't you think?"

If Two-Gun Billy said anything she didn't hear it. His face was turned away, buried against the sofa.

9

The voices reached Milo as if through a dream.

"You mean to tell me that kid's back there in my sleeper? Nice of you to wait until we were out on the road before saying anything. I have a good mind to toss the both of you out right now."

"I'm sorry, Curtis, but he was still passed out and I knew we had to get moving. I didn't know what else to do."

All was dark, except for a crack of light in what seemed to be a curtain. Milo tried to sit up but his body was obedient only to the slight rolling and pitching that shuddered through him.

"Man, I can't get over that scar. You're saying that kid back there did that?"

"He didn't give me the scar. He just ... he stopped the bleeding anyway."

"Look at the size of that thing. What did he have, a foot-long bandage?"

"Of course not. Everything happened kind of fast."

That was Mavis Jean's voice, but Milo didn't recognize the man. He realized he was in a truck, being hauled like cargo, like one of the cattle carcasses in his dreams. That's how he felt. Opened up and flattened out.

"I saw that huge stain on the parking lot. That wasn't motor oil, girl. I still say we should have called the police or at least taken you to a hospital."

The voice wasn't Ned's or that other one with the knife. Milo remembered the screeching of tires, the flash of headlights, then kneeling over Mavis Jean.

So much blood.

"As you can see, I don't need a doctor. And I already talked to the police. I wasn't pressing charges. I wanted to hit the road, pronto."

It had taken all his concentration, every inch of his being to force back that flood. He had never extended himself like that before. The mere memory of it was enough to push him towards unconsciousness, but his mind ebbed back to St. Tom's where he first discovered this secret part of himself. He was loath to call it a power, because it usually ended up draining him of his energy. A gift? A talent? A curse? A blessing? None of these terms seemed satisfactory. For Milo it was more like a muscle that had lain dormant. A hidden sinew uniting mental, physical and possibly even spiritual aspects of himself.

"I don't know, Mavis Jean. I still got a feeling you're not telling me everything. Why'd you have to go and put that kid in my sleeper?"

"His name is Milo. After that asshole slashed me and took off with his buddy, Milo tried to help me. Then everything went black. When I woke up he was passed out. I couldn't just leave him there."

"What'd the police say about all that?"

"Nothing. It was too complicated to explain. That's why I dragged him into the sleeper before they showed up."

"At least we're somewhere closer to the truth now."

"Look, Curtis, I'm not trying to hide anything from you. I'm telling you everything I know."

"I think you're telling me everything you think I need to know. Like you did to the police. I think you don't really trust me."

"I wouldn't be riding with you if I didn't trust you."

"Then maybe it's me who shouldn't be trusting you, girl."

Lying here like this in the dark, listening to other voices, reminded Milo of lights out at St. Tom's. Even the sense of movement. Back in his little iron bed there was always a hint of motion that came with staying absolutely still. Trying to feel how the earth turns was one way of forgetting his loneliness. Imagining the whole world moving together at the same time, to the same celestial rhythm. Listening to the whimpering, sobbing and snoring all around him, he would touch each of his fingertips to his lips over and over (similar to the way his grandmother kissed her rosary) until he fell asleep.

"I guess what's really bothering me, Mavis Jean, is the way you took my keys and snuck out in the middle of the night."

"But I needed to get something from my duffel bag."

"What?" he asked.

"This."

"A Bible? Are you kidding me? I never took you for no kind of holy roller."

"I ain't. But I always found comfort in it ever since I was a kid."

"Yeah, whatever."

"There's this game I play," she explained. "I ask a question, then I close my eyes, turn to any page and point to a passage. And whatever it says, that's the answer to my question. Wanna try it?"

"It's a holy book, Mavis Jean, not a Ouija board."

"Man, you sound just like my Aunt Vesta."

"I'm glad you find that funny," he said.

"Fine, I'll do it. *Am I doing the right thing in bringing Milo home with me?*"

"I didn't know you were bringing him home with you."

"Whadja think, we were gonna dump him off at the next gas station?" She sighed impatiently. "Now, I close my eyes, open to a page and point to a passage."

The engine grew louder and Milo strained to hear. When the engine settled back into its regular rumble Curtis spoke.

"Well, you gonna read it to me or what?"

"*But the father said to his servants, bring forth the best robe, and put it on him; and put a ring on his hand, and shoes on his feet: And bring hither the fatted calf, and kill it; and let us eat, and be merry. For this my son was dead, and is alive again; he was lost, and is found.*"

"So what's that supposed to mean?"

"Isn't it obvious? It's telling me I'm doing the right thing."

"You really believe that?"

"You calling the Bible a liar? Anyway, it's only meant to be a game."

Milo was aware of something strange in her voice. A slight agitation, as if the Bible's answer was not what she had expected. At that moment the far end of the curtain opened and Mavis Jean stuck her head in. Milo shielded his eyes from the light's brightness. After a moment he could make out the snaky scar along her neck.

"Hey there," she said, almost too cheerfully. "You awake?"

10

Two-Gun Billy couldn't sleep.

He lay bundled under his horse blanket in the sleeping compartment in the back of the truck cab. He'd been driving with White Line

Express for about a month now and didn't have any money to waste on some motel. The semi was parked off to the side of the highway, somewhere between Drumheller and Calgary. He was hauling a trailer filled with machine parts.

A reckless wind was rattling the windows and whistling through the exhaust pipes. He listened to its piercing anguish, a wounded animal begging to be put out of its misery. The heater was broken and the mattress hard, not to mention this sleeper was as narrow as a coffin. He couldn't move his legs or his arms. They were numb from the cold. With some effort he raised his right hand to scratch his nose. It felt like the tip of an iceberg. He breathed against his cupped palm to generate a bit of warmth.

Despite this discomfort, he felt safe. Out in the middle of nowhere he could forget the world. Once he saw a science fiction movie on the late show where invaders from outer space threatened to destroy everyone on the planet. He really didn't like the movie much, but every so often he imagined that something like that did happen and he was the last person left alive. Living in an empty world seemed to be the only possible way to start afresh.

He listened to the wind hammering against his rig and imagined that its persistent wailing originated from somewhere inside him. He thought of his two pearl-handled six-shooters cradled in their hand-tooled leather holsters somewhere in the attic. After the botched-up incident with the penknife, Vesta was afraid of what he might do with them. He didn't care. He never wanted to see or touch those things again. That part of his life was definitely over now.

He was glad to be on the road. Cold and lonely perhaps, but glad all the same to be away from the house. Away from Vesta and all her weeping and apologizing. She would be going to Edmonton for a spell before anybody noticed the change in her. She promised him that she would take care of everything. He didn't need to worry. It would be like nothing ever happened.

This was the sole thought he concentrated on as he listened to the raging wind. Here, wedged in this coffin-like sleeping compartment, he could believe that nothing had ever happened.

He rubbed the tip of his nose, trying to stop the numbness in his legs and arm from spreading. Then he let the hand rest over where he thought his heart should be. It too seemed to have stopped frozen like a rusty old watch spring. He closed his eyes and let the troubled wind sing him to sleep.

11

"How long has he been sleeping on the sofa?"

Mavis Jean sat at one end of the kitchen table while Vesta, still in her dressing gown, poured three mugs of coffee at the other end. Milo sat quietly between the two women, almost an invisible presence, the way a child is among adults.

"Almost a week now," said Vesta as she placed steaming mugs in front of Mavis Jean and Milo and added spoons as afterthoughts. "There's milk and sugar on the table. Unless you'd prefer Sweet'N Low."

"This is fine." Mavis Jean spooned three sugars into hers and added a splash of milk. "Don't you think he'd be better off in a hospital or a nursing home? It can't be easy for you to take care of him like this."

"This is where he wants to be."

"I thought he didn't know where he was half the time."

"It would be worse in a hospital," said Vesta with an air of authority. "He needs familiar surroundings."

"I hope the doorbell did not wake him up," said Milo.

Both women turned suddenly, as if toward a disembodied voice.

"After this last stroke they changed his medication," Vesta explained. "It makes him sleep more. Sometimes it's hard to get him up in the morning. Of course that gives me a bit of a break."

"You look like you need one," said Mavis Jean.

Vesta rose from her chair and went to the fridge. "You both must be hungry. I could make you some eggs. Or maybe a nice stack of pancakes?"

"Not for me," said Mavis Jean.

"No thank you," said Milo.

Vesta stared at the perfect row of eggs sitting so white and innocent in their plastic holders on the inside of the fridge door. She shut it and resumed her seat. "You still haven't told me how you got that nasty scar on your neck."

"Just some bad luck. Being in the wrong place at the wrong time, that's all."

"She was trying to help me," Milo said.

"Never mind that." She took a deep breath and rubbed her eyes. "The point is Milo helped me. That's why I brought him here."

Vesta looked from Mavis Jean to Milo.

"I think he might be able to help my daddy," said Mavis Jean.

"How?" asked Vesta.

"He can heal." Mavis Jean edged closer to Milo. "Isn't that right?"

He looked down at his hands. "If I knew that is why you brought me here ..."

"What are you talking about?" said Vesta.

"He saved my life. Didn't you?" Irritation was creeping into Mavis Jean's voice.

"You were bleeding," Milo said. He turned to Vesta. "I only wanted to help."

"Don't you want to help now? My daddy is dying in there."

"Let the boy be," said Vesta. "There's nothing any of us can do for your daddy now except keep him comfortable."

"That's easy for you to say. You're used to watching him get worse."

"I devoted myself to him," said Vesta.

"He should be in a hospital, not on the sofa."

"That's not for you to say. You have no right." Vesta covered her mouth.

"You mean because I ran away?" Mavis Jean challenged Vesta with an unwavering look.

"That's not what I was going to say."

"See this?" Mavis Jean craned her neck, the better to show the scar. "It was gushing blood until this one put his hands on me and the wound closed."

Vesta turned to Milo. "Is this true?"

Milo said nothing and tried to hide his hands in his lap. Mavis Jean smacked her hand on the table so hard the spoons jumped. "Go ahead, tell her!"

"You need to calm down now," said Vesta.

Milo's only response was to start touching the tips of each finger to his lips. His eyes were closed. To Vesta it looked like he was praying.

"Stop that!" Mavis Jean grabbed Milo by the wrists, pinning his hands against the table. "I need you to back me up here."

"Let go of him," said Vesta.

"You saved my life, didn't you? Tell her!"

"I will not have this sort of behaviour in my house."

Mavis Jean let go of Milo's hands and turned away from both of them.

"I am sorry," said Milo, rubbing his wrists.

"You're not the one who should be apologizing," said Vesta sympathetically.

Mavis Jean drank the last of her coffee and took the empty mug to the sink.

"Are you alright?" Vesta asked Milo as she cleared the rest of the table.

"So very sorry," he repeated, then rose from his seat and left the kitchen.

Vesta needed to wash and dress before Two-Gun Billy woke up, so Mavis Jean decided to step out onto the porch for a cigarette. Milo sat on one of the lower steps writing in his notebook.

The sun slowly rose from behind Dale Cochrane's silo, lighting the top of it like a birthday candle. Thin wispy clouds underlined the blankness of the sky, the brilliance of its blue pure as an infant's gaze.

"I'm sorry about what happened back there." Two lazy streams of smoke escaped through her nostrils. "I hope I didn't hurt you."

He continued writing.

"I don't think I ever thanked you properly for what you did back in Dauphin. I most likely would've bled to death." She lowered her head so the brim of her hat blocked the sun's glare. "Thank you."

His pen hesitated for a moment, but then started scribbling again like it had a mind of its own and his hand was merely attached.

"Look, Milo, I don't blame you for being mad at me."

"I am not mad," he said without stopping or looking up.

"It's really strange for me to be back here. It's been five years but it feels like no time has passed at all."

She glanced at Two-Gun Billy's empty chair.

"When I think of all the hours I spent sitting in the passenger seat of somebody or other's rig. It's like those were frozen hours retreating into some inner part of myself. Half the time I couldn't tell whether I was running away from something or heading toward it."

Milo stopped writing, closed his notebook and slipped the pen into the spiral binding. "I know that feeling."

She stared at the back of his head, that mess of orange corkscrews springing out from under his bandana, and had the feeling that he was looking straight at her without turning around.

"But last night I had a sense that I was moving toward something," he said. "It was during another dream about the slaughtered cattle. This one was different from the others. In this dream the carcasses were strewn everywhere, draped over large boulders and hanging from limbs of trees. It was cold and I wrapped a carcass around me like a blanket. I think it was still warm with the dead animal's heat. At first it felt loose, like a robe. But then it formed right onto my body. Even my head was covered and I was looking through the empty eye sockets."

"What was that like?" she asked. "Looking out through strange eyeholes?"

"I felt like I had found myself. Or at least a part of myself that I had lost."

"I'd give anything to feel that."

She moved down and sat beside him.

"I remember one time me and Two-Gun Billy were hauling a load of grain to a mill in Lethbridge. Along the number 24 highway we saw a cab and its trailer turned over in a ditch off the road. We slowed down for a better look, but there weren't no one else around, no driver, no cops, nothing. Just that hunk of machine lying on its side, abandoned. I remember the stillness of those huge tires suspended in the air. And the underbelly of struts and axles exposed to the elements, just waiting to get all rusted and useless. Two-Gun Billy took a long hard look as we passed and shook his head. I asked him if anybody would be coming back for it. He only shrugged. 'Maybe to strip it for parts.' he said. 'Like buzzards on an old carcass.' Then he hammered down like he couldn't get away fast enough. It was like the sight of that rig scared the hell outta him. I never saw him like that before."

To her surprise, Mavis Jean found that she was clutching Milo's hand. It was clear to her that this made him feel uncomfortable but she held on.

"I'm asking you—no, begging you—to please help Two-Gun Billy."

"I wish I could," he said, unable to look right at her. "But it is beyond me."

"How do you know? You ain't even tried."

"Sorry," he said and slipped his hand out of her grasp. "I know I am letting you down."

The front door opened and Vesta stepped out onto the porch.

"He's awake," she said.

12

He stared at the three figures standing before him. Vesta took a step forward while the other two stood behind. They didn't look like doctors or nurses, so he most likely wasn't in the hospital. No, they looked more like gravediggers. Maybe even grave robbers, too impatient to wait until he was dead and buried. Whoever they were he didn't trust their faces.

"Bill, see who's here." said Vesta. "Mavis Jean is back home."

He searched the hard angles of the girl's face. Youthful but weathered. Some resemblance to Vesta.

"It's me, Daddy." She got down on one knee so they were eye-level.

A rippling memory swam around his brain like a goldfish circling inside a glass bowl for the hundredth time: him sitting in the kitchen in his undershirt, shivering, with oatmeal everywhere.

"Where my shir'?"

She turned to Vesta. "He still remembers?"

"Mavis Jean doesn't have your shirt, Bill. She's been away all this time."

"I been to some of the old places we used to stop at, Daddy," Mavis Jean said, hoping to win him over.

His attention was distracted by the third figure pulling the bandana off his head, unleashing a wild crown of flaming curls. Two-Gun Billy sucked air into the crooked slit of his mouth.

"Daddy? You okay?"

"His back might be hurting him," said Vesta. "Would you like to sit up, Bill?"

He dismissed both of them with a wave. "G'way!"

He was mesmerized by the unruly red hair the way Moses must have been confronting the burning bush. Two-Gun Billy motioned for the young man to come closer.

"That's Milo," said Mavis Jean. "He's from Toronto."

"Don' be 'fraid." Two-Gun Billy stretched his crooked mouth into something resembling a smile.

"He wants you to go over to him," said Vesta.

The young man went over and towered above like a fiery morning star.

"I am Milo."

Two-Gun Billy's rigid mouth began to tremble. "My ... low ...."

"Very good, Bill," said Vesta.

The young man grinned timidly. "I am pleased to meet you."

"Howz you mama?"

"What?" said Mavis Jean. She turned to Vesta. "What's Daddy talking about?"

"Bill, you don't know this boy," said Vesta with annoyance. "Why you asking after his mother?"

"I just brought him here, Daddy. I brought him here to help you."

"Now listen to me, Bill. You don't know this boy."

"My ... low ..." said Two-Gun Billy. "He my son."

"What?" cried Mavis Jean.

"No, Bill, he is not your son," Vesta said sharply. "You don't have a son. You have a daughter. Mavis Jean. Remember?"

"He knows that," Mavis Jean said. "He knows his own flesh and blood."

Two-Gun Billy kept staring at the red-haired young man. "Lynesse boy. My boy."

"No, Bill. He is not Lynette's boy."

"I'm your daughter!" Mavis Jean rose to her full height. "Don't you recognize me?"

Two-Gun Billy gave Milo's hand a weak squeeze and closed his eyes. When he opened his eyes the young man and the other one were gone. Only Vesta stood there with her arms crossed like she was coatless in sub-zero weather.

13

Inside Two-Gun Billy's room the cedar smell Mavis Jean remembered as a child was replaced by something else, reminding her of when you remove a cast from a broken arm, the way the air first hits peeling dead skin and suffocating pores. A grey smell, like the grimy inside of old plaster and gauze. She opened the window.

She turned on the lamp with the green shade then turned it off again. How many times had she seen that eerie glow in her mind whenever she closed her eyes in some strange room? She sat on the stripped-down bed.

The door opened.

Vesta lingered for a moment before finally entering. The two women surveyed the room in an effort to avoid looking at each other.

"He'd probably be more comfortable up here," said Vesta, gazing at his boots in the corner of the closet. "Maybe you and Milo could carry him up."

"It was his absence that always had the claim on this room."

"You mustn't take what he said to heart."

Vesta joined Mavis Jean on the edge of the bed. The two of them sitting there like that made Mavis Jean feel self-conscious. "What's all this about a son? That the stroke talking? Or the medication?"

Vesta was quiet for a moment. When she finally did speak it was almost a whisper. "The truth of it is he does have a son. At least he believes he does."

Mavis Jean felt something swirling in the pit of her stomach.

"Lynette got pregnant early," Vesta continued. "They had to get married."

"I already knew that. She was pregnant with me."

Vesta lowered her head and wrapped her wiry arms around her flat breasts. "We don't know if she had a boy. Even so he'd be your half-brother."

"You said she died after giving birth to me."

"That seemed to be the easiest explanation. Truth is she left your daddy for another man. Some big shot from Toronto. She was about four months along."

"You're not making any sense."

"Your daddy was devastated when she left. I didn't know how to help him. At first he was going to find her and kill her. But he knew he could never do that. He would just fall on his knees and beg her to come back. He actually did take a train to Toronto, but all he did was drink until he got beat up and robbed one night. I had to wire him the money so he could come back home."

Mavis Jean heard the words but had trouble connecting them to the woman in front of her. It was as if Aunt Vesta's mouth was moving but someone else was doing the talking, an invisible ventriloquist. These were not Aunt Vesta's words.

"When he returned he went through a dark period, lying in his room for days on end, hardly touching food but drinking a whole lot. One afternoon I found water under the bathroom door. It was red. He had cut his wrists with a penknife and passed out in the bath from too much whiskey. Luckily the cuts weren't too deep and he bled out less than he might otherwise have if he'd known what he was doing. I bandaged him myself. I knew there would have to be an inquiry if I took him to the hospital. He might have been declared a danger to himself and maybe put away somewhere. But he wasn't a danger to himself. He was only grieving."

"You still haven't told me when she gave birth to me?" Mavis Jean rubbed her palms nervously. "I used to like looking at the pictures of her in the photo album. She looked so beautiful in her costume."

"Thing is," said Vesta, "I could see that he was fading away from the world. It frightened me."

"I kept thinking how she was dead. In those photos she was frozen in time, like a beautiful butterfly pressed between the pages of a book."

"I was desperate, you see," Vesta said, partially to herself. "I needed to pull him back in somehow."

Mavis Jean felt a wave of bitterness wash through her. "Well, isn't that just like you? So selfless. So strong."

"What do you mean?"

"Aunt Vesta the martyr. Aunt Vesta the saint."

"How dare you say such things. You don't know ..."

Mavis Jean looked her straight in the eye. "I remember how you hated it when he took me on the road with him."

"No!" Vesta protested.

"And after he couldn't drive anymore? I couldn't bear to see him like that day after day. But you couldn't get enough of it."

"That's a terrible thing to say. You don't know what I went through." Vesta stared down at her hands. "I only wanted to be an instrument of mercy."

Mavis Jean watched the slow ravage of tears. "When did my mother give birth to me?"

"It started off very innocent." Vesta passed a sleeve across her red eyes. "I just lay down beside him at first. Just to comfort him."

Mavis Jean was suddenly aware of how close they were sitting.

"What in hell are you saying to me?"

Vesta rose from the bed and stood in the middle of the room.

"When I realized I was ... with child, I knew we had to keep it secret. I went off to Edmonton to get myself taken care of. But I couldn't go through with it. And I'm not sorry I couldn't."

"I don't want to hear any more."

"Your daddy was mad at first when I brought you back. But he accepted you. You filled the emptiness in him. I swore to him that we'd never tell you."

Mavis Jean could feel the blood draining from her face. She looked toward the bedroom door. It seemed so remote, a threshold to the faraway past. The distance of it exhausted her.

"I never meant to hurt you," said Vesta.

Mavis Jean managed to get to her feet. "You're a lying bitch!" She slapped Vesta across the face.

Mavis Jean's hand stung as she grabbed the door handle and stumbled out into the hallway. With every step she imagined a cold pit of darkness waiting below and fully expected the floorboards to collapse beneath her. It was almost a disappointment when they didn't.

Once inside her room, she slammed the door behind her and heard footsteps retreating down the stairwell. Her duffel bag sat at the foot of her bed, not yet unpacked. Her first inclination was to hoist it onto her shoulder, head down to the highway and stick her thumb out.

She took the travelling Bible out of the duffel bag and slowly tugged the zipper along the edges, rounding each corner until it fell open before she could even ask a question. Immediately she extended an index finger and pointed to a passage from the Gospel of John 13:33. *My children, I will be with you only a little longer. You will look for me, and just as I told the Jews, so I tell you now: Where I am going, you cannot come.*

She looked up and saw the square part of the ceiling that led to the attic directly above her room. She had rarely gone up there.

She dragged a chair over and stood on it. Just the right height. She pushed with both hands and lifted the wooden square from its groove, moving it aside. A musty smell wafted down. She imagined the cobwebs and dust that must have accumulated after so many years. No matter, she knew there were things up there she wanted to see. With some effort she pulled herself up into the darkness.

14

The first page of the album showed a photograph of a woman dressed up in a spangled blouse, matching short skirt and tasselled cowboy boots. She had thick red hair cascading from beneath a white Stetson and long shapely legs. Both hands were perched on hips with slender fingers splayed against the skirt and bent elbows forming sharp symmetrical angles. It was a pose both defiant and seductive. But what interested Milo was the expression on her face. While the eyes stared boldly at the camera, there was tension around the pouting mouth. Clearly she was trying to exude sex appeal, but there was also the sense that she was suppressing something. Laughter perhaps. Or possibly tears.

He was sitting on the floor by the sofa with the album propped against raised knees. Two-Gun Billy was asleep. His breathing whistled in Milo's ear.

"Those are pictures of Lynette," said Vesta as she entered the living room carrying a tray with pills and water. "See the flaming red hair? That's why he thinks you're her son."

"Neither of my parents have red hair. My father was blond. He was a merchant marine. And my mother is dark. She has spent most of her time in and out of hospitals. I was raised by my grandmother. Her hair is mostly grey, although I think it was reddish brown as a child."

"Sometimes it skips a generation."

Milo closed the album and returned it to the credenza. Vesta set the tray on the floor by the sofa and knelt down, gently shaking her brother's shoulder.

"Come on. Wake up, Bill. Time for your pills."

Milo went to the window so Vesta could administer the medicine. Parting the blinds, he discovered a world of impenetrable night, except for a dimly lit window at the Cochrane farm across the road. No stars. No moon. He thought he could hear the sound of cattle out there in the darkness.

"Do you believe in the power of dreams?"

"What do you mean by power?" said Vesta.

"That they have meaning and are connected to one's destiny."

"I think destiny is something that's in your hands rather than in your head."

He listened again for the lowing cattle but only heard Two-Gun Billy's raspy sputtering as he was slowly aroused to consciousness. Milo watched Vesta shake pills out of a series of plastic containers. She patiently placed a pill in Two-Gun Billy's hand so he could take it himself and held the glass of water near so he could drink from the bendable straw to wash down the pill. She did this with each pill he had to take, around ten in all. When he was done he laid his head back down. Vesta set the tray on top of the credenza.

"All that business Mavis Jean was saying this morning, about you being able to heal. What did she mean?"

"I can make wounds close with my bare hands."

"How is that possible?"

He showed his open palms as if for inspection. "I do not know."

"Is it like you can feel God healing through you?"

"I am not sure I would exactly call it healing."

"Then what would you call it?" asked Mavis Jean.

She descended the staircase wearing a white Stetson with spangled blouse, matching skirt and tasselled cowboy boots that Milo recognized as the same outfit he'd seen Lynette wearing in the photo album. Around her waist was the hand-tooled leather gun belt with two holsters. She held Two-Gun Billy's old pearl-handled revolvers in each hand.

"Put those things away," said Vesta. "You don't know if they're loaded."

"They are." Mavis Jean twirled one of the pistols once around an index finger and managed to catch the grip in her palm.

Vesta winced. "Be careful, that thing's liable to go off."

"With a bit of practice I might be a regular chip off the old block." She showed off the cold gleam of their long stainless steel barrels. "Spent the last couple of hours cleaning these up. They're still in mint condition. Even found an unopened box of bullets."

She slid one pistol sideways along the length of her forearm. The spinning cylinder made a clean clicking noise like a tiny roulette wheel. "Music to my ears."

"I want you to stop this foolishness now!" said Vesta.

Mavis Jean cocked both hammers and pointed the revolvers at Milo. "You didn't answer my question. If being able to close wounds with your bare hands isn't healing, then what is it?"

Milo did what he could to ignore the guns and focused his attention on Mavis Jean's face. The serious expression in her eyes did little to calm his nerves. He felt an unnatural stillness creeping into his bones.

"The first time I discovered this part of myself was back at St. Tom's when I saved one of the older patients from suicide. I had found him bleeding in the showers. He broke open a plastic disposable razor and used the blade to slash his wrists. I grabbed him by the wrists and tried to get him to stand up. Then I felt a strange warmth concentrated in different parts of myself—between my eyes, at the back of my neck, in my belly and across my knuckles. For some reason I kept squeezing his wrists until he was screaming so much I was forced to let go. When the orderlies came he held out his wrists and showed them purple scars where moments ago there had been open slits leaking blood."

"This was in some kind of a hospital?" asked Vesta.

"A mental hospital," snapped Mavis Jean. "That don't mean nothing."

"I knew I had somehow mended that patient's wounds and admitted as much to Dr. Veldt. He was afraid that I had developed some form of schizophrenia. Up to that point I was in St. Tom's voluntarily, but Dr. Veldt wanted me committed. Before my status could be changed in the Admissions Office, I slipped out as naturally as if I was going for a newspaper."

"What does some headshrinker know?" said Mavis Jean. "You have a gift for healing. You perform miracles."

"Even though I saved that man from his wounds I could not stop him from wanting to commit suicide. While they were taking him up to the Chronic Ward he threw himself down a flight of stairs and died. You see, what I do is quick and superficial. Healing takes longer."

"Well, my daddy doesn't have time on his side." She aimed both barrels at Milo's heart. "If quick and superficial are all you got, then they'll have to do."

"I do not know where to start," Milo pleaded.

"Doesn't matter." She waved him toward Two-Gun Billy. "Go."

Vesta stood in his way. "I'm not letting either of you near him."

"Stand aside." Mavis Jean pointed a pistol at her.

"I will not be threatened in my own house."

Mavis Jean fired into the living room ceiling. The abrupt bang echoed in Milo's ears. Vesta covered her head as bits of plaster rained down.

"Now get over there," said Mavis Jean.

"What can I do?" Milo threw up his hands. "He has no external wounds."

"Whaddya mean?" asked Mavis Jean.

"I only know how to close up wounds. He has no wounds for me to close up."

Mavis Jean hesitated. "Forgive me, Daddy."

She aimed one pistol and shot her father in the forearm. The withered appendage jumped in reflex like a stick. Immediately blood spurted out of the wound and streamed down his wrist and through his gnarled fingers, staining the sofa and rug. His eyes widened at the sight and he began to howl. Vesta collapsed onto her knees. "No!"

"But I shot him in the paralyzed arm." Mavis Jean trained both barrels at Milo once more. "There's your wound. Now fix him up."

Milo was covered in blood. He felt his knees buckle, but he was able to brace himself against the wall. His eyes widened, yet seemed not to be looking at anything. He systematically touched each of his fingertips to his lips, muttering something under his breath.

"Don't you crap out on me now," said Mavis Jean. "My daddy needs help. You have to help him."

Two-Gun Billy's mouth was opened in a lopsided oval, emitting a sound that seemed to reverberate from something hollow and endless. An echo originating from an age-old cry.

"Shoot me if you want," warned Vesta. "But I'm not going to just do nothing."

"Somebody fix him up!" A quaver of fear crept into Mavis Jean's voice. She still held the pistols aloft but aimed at no one in particular.

Vesta strode past Mavis Jean toward the downstairs bathroom and quickly returned with a first-aid kit. She knelt down by Two-Gun Billy and inspected his arm.

"What a mess," she said and turned to Mavis Jean. "Put those things down and help me."

Mavis Jean merely stared at her.

"Now!" cried Vesta. "There's no time to waste."

Mavis Jean holstered the pistols and knelt beside Vesta. "I don't know what to do."

"Just do everything I tell you. Open up that kit and hand me the bottle of alcohol. Then cut some bandages, about thirty centimetres long, from that roll of gauze."

Mavis Jean helplessly held out a roll of gauze. "How am I s'posed know how long that is?"

"Just make them as long as your arm." Vesta looked her in the eye. "It'll be okay."

Mavis Jean did as she was told, using slender steel scissors to snip the gauze from the roll while Vesta wrapped Two-Gun Billy's arm and fastened the bandage with a small triangular metal clasp. Soon Two-Gun Billy's arm was resting in an improvised sling made from torn strips of an old bed sheet.

Both women were suddenly aware of something, a sound that seemed to haunt the air. They turned their attention to Milo who was still crouched against the wall. He had not stopped kissing his fingertips, the whole time repeating something under his breath.

"What is he saying?" asked Vesta.

Mavis Jean tilted her head towards him. "Not too sure."

They listened closely until they could make out the words.

"*For this my son was dead, and is alive again; he was lost, and is found,*" repeated Milo over and over to himself.

15

The first sliver of morning sun found Mavis Jean sitting on the porch in Two-Gun Billy's rattan chair. She hadn't been to bed and was still wearing the spangled outfit. Tasselled boots were propped up on the metal railing. The air carried some of the night's chill and her thin bare legs and bony arms were pocked with goose pimples. The white Stetson sat on a small table. Next to it Two-Gun Billy's leather gun belt was rolled up with the six-shooters snug in their holsters. The zippered travelling Bible sat in her lap.

She rolled a cigarette. Milo stepped out onto the porch with his backpack.

"Going somewhere?" asked Mavis Jean.

Milo set the backpack down on the top porch step. "Thank you for letting me sleep in your room. I am feeling a bit better."

"Get some breakfast in you?"

"Yes. And your aunt made sandwiches to take with me."

Mavis Jean winced at the word *aunt* but did not bother to correct him.

He hunched his shoulders and jammed his hands into his front pockets for warmth. The sky was just starting to open itself up to the world.

"Strange," said Mavis Jean. "No matter how wide-open or how blue and cloudless, no matter how empty it looks, I always get the feeling the sky is hiding more than it's revealing."

Milo yawned. "What will you do now?"

Mavis Jean opened the travelling Bible and read aloud: "*This is what the Lord says: 'David will never fail to have a man to sit on the throne of the house of Israel, nor will the priests, who are Levites, ever fail to have a man to stand before me continually to offer burnt offerings, to burn grain offerings and to present sacrifices.'*"

She listened to the sound of motors in the distance, the early morning traffic barrelling along Highway 9.

"Originally, Vesta bought this Bible for Two-Gun Billy to take on the road. But he never had any use for a Bible, so she hid it in the bottom drawer of the bedside table in his room. Since he spent more time on the road than at home, it was more like one of them Gideon Bibles they put in the hotel rooms. That's how Vesta explained it, anyway. She figured what he didn't know wouldn't hurt him.

"I used to go into his room and play my question-and-answer game with it until Vesta caught me. She told me the Bible was meant for comfort and guidance, not some kinda fortune-telling device. Far as I was concerned I was using it for guidance, to find out when Two-Gun Billy was going to take me on his next haul. But she said that was no excuse for abusing the Holy Book and that nothing is guaranteed. She said all our faith lies in the mysteries of life.

"After that I was forbidden to go into Two-Gun Billy's room. There was another Bible in the house, but I liked this one, maybe because it was associated with travelling, with movement and change. I was convinced it told the truth. I used to take it along whenever I got to go with Two-Gun Billy on the road. He didn't mind playing the game with me during long stretches behind the wheel.

"But when I had to stay home I'd sneak into his empty room in the middle of the night, so that I could get into the bottom drawer of the bedside table and ask this Bible all the questions that preyed on my mind during the day. Being there in his room under the green-shaded lamp made me feel like my body didn't exist anymore. Something in me vibrated and hummed with pure energy. I felt like it was my soul coming alive."

She zipped up the travelling Bible and tossed it to Milo. He pulled his hands out of his pockets in time to catch it and turned it over and over, studying the scuffed leather cover with a mystified expression.

"Why are you giving this to me?"

"Why do ya think? It's meant for travelling, ain't it?"

Mavis Jean squashed her cigarette in the ashtray and started to roll another. Milo slipped the Bible into his backpack, then hefted the pack onto his shoulders and clomped down the porch steps.

She called out to him: "Still thinking of heading to Oyen?"

He raised a hand in farewell, not looking back as he strode down the walkway to the narrow road. Mavis Jean watched as he made his way toward the highway. Long after he disappeared from view she was still rolling one cigarette after another, smoking and staring at the roadside littered with dusty pebbles like they were the skeletons of burnt-out stars.

ACKNOWLEDGEMENTS

Thanks to the following (in no particular order) for their patience, honesty, tough love, cool vibes and general support and encouragement: Robin Enns, Marjorie MacDonald, Paula Wing, Thelma Phillips, Vivian Phillips, Rena Mayoff, Richard Cumyn, The Maritime Writers' Workshop, Sasha Fligel, J. J. Steinfeld, Alistair MacLeod, The Great Blue Heron Writing Workshop, Wayne Tefs and all the hardworking folks at Turnstone Press.

Earlier versions of these stories originally appeared in the following publications: "The Same Machine" in *Front&Centre*; "Home, James" in *Upstairs At Duroc*; "Forgiveness" in *All Rights Reserved*; "Fatted Calf Blues" in *Vocabula Review*; "The Darkened Door" in *The Windsor Review*; "The Two Annes" in *Grimm Magazine*; "The Animal Room" in *The Dublin Quarterly*; "The Most Important Man in the World" in *filling Station*; "Elephant Rock" in *Forget Magazine*; "The Bridge by Moonlight" in *The Dalhousie Review*; "Smoke and Mirrors" in *Pottersfield Portfolio*; "Danger in the Summer Moon Above" in *Grain*.